Single
to
Center

Single to Center

by Bill J. Carol

Steck-Vaughn Company,
An Intext *Publisher*
Austin, Texas

This book is dedicated to a fine ballplayer,
Judy Knott.

Library of Congress Cataloging in Publication Data

Knott, Bill, 1927–
  Single to Center.

  SUMMARY: An eleven-year-old boy has to work out the problem of having
his sister play on the Little League team while he sits on the bench.
  [1. Baseball—Fiction. 2. Brothers and sisters—Fiction] I. Title.
PZ7.K755Si   [Fic]   73–21921
ISBN 0–8114–7763–0

ISBN 0–8114–7763–0
Library of Congress Catalog Card Number 73–21921

OTHER SPORTS BOOKS BY BILL J. CAROL

1

MIKE STARED OUT the window of his room at the unfamiliar street below him.

He wondered bleakly if he would ever get used to living in a large town. He was still haunted by memories of Sterling Valley, the pleasant little village where he had lived for most of his eleven years. When he closed his eyes at night he would again see Sterling Valley's tree-lined streets and the wide, shaded lawns —and be filled with an ache that would not let him sleep.

There was no sense of warmth in this town of Addison. A strangeness was all he felt, that and a sense that he could never really belong.

A soft knock on his door broke into his gloomy reverie. He turned from the window and called, "Come in."

His sister, Jean, opened the door and stood in the doorway. Mike noticed that she had just braided her pigtails and that a bat rested lightly on one shoulder. Jean had on her baseball cap, and her glove was hanging from the bat handle. "What are you doing all cooped up in here?" she asked him.

"You wouldn't understand, Sis," Mike said, turning away from her to look back out the window.

"Come on," Jean said. "I found a neat place, a small park down the street. It's even got base lines and a backstop. Get your glove."

"I don't feel like it."

"You'd rather sulk up here. Is that it?"

"What would you know about it?" Mike turned to look at his sister scornfully. "Sometimes I don't think you have any feelings at all. All you want to do is play baseball."

"And all you want to do is feel sorry for yourself. You're turning into a real moper."

Mike sprang to his feet and faced her. "Hey! You better take that back!"

"Or you'll what."

"You know what."

She smiled suddenly. "Okay. I take it back. And now that you've come back to life, let's go. It's a real neat park. Honest!"

Mike felt himself wavering. But he didn't see how it could be such a neat park in this town. "You go ahead. I have already told you I don't feel like it."

"You will when you see what I have."

"What do you have?"

"I'm not going to tell you unless you get your glove and come on."

"What is it?"

"Something Dad gave me. He said it might cheer you up." She looked at him coldly for a minute. "But I told him I didn't think anything could do that."

Mike took a step toward her. "Okay. Show me."

Jean brought a hand forward that she had been holding behind her and opened it to show a new baseball. Mike hurried to her and took the ball in his hands. He tossed it to see how much it weighed. It felt light.

"It's regulation," his sister said. "See what it says on the cover."

Mike read it and looked back up at his sister. "Official National League!"

"Imagine how far we can hit that!" she said.

At once Mike lost all his reluctance. Only once or twice in the past had he ever had a new baseball to hit; most of the time they had used old ones he and his sister had had to tape again and again.

3

"Okay," said Mike, heading for the corner where his bat was leaning against the wall, his glove on the floor beside it, "but I bat first."

"No, you don't!" she cried, darting ahead of him down the stairs. "We'll toss for it!"

He slammed the door and hurried down the stairs after Jean, realizing that that was indeed what they would end up doing. But he would find himself a real flat stone.

Mike tossed the ball into the air, strode forward, and swung—catching the ball on the fat part of the bat. The ball rose swiftly toward the deepest part of the ball park, but Jean was already on the way. In full gallop, she reached up and speared the baseball. Pulling up casually, Jean turned around and trotted in, a pleased smile on her face.

"Nice catch, Sis," Mike said, as he picked up his glove and trotted out past her.

"You bet it was," she replied, grinning at him. "Now watch how far I poke it."

"Bet you can't get it over the trees."

"You watch."

Jean's first hit to him was a low liner. He caught it on the first bounce. She placed her bat down and stepped back. He threw carefully, and it looked as if

4

the ball were going to strike the bat; but at the last moment, it hopped over the handle.

"Too bad!" Mike's sister called to him as she took up the bat again.

"Over the trees!" he said. "Go ahead!"

She tossed the ball and stepped up quickly, swinging as hard as she could. The ball began to rise fast, but Mike had his eye on it. At first, judging this new baseball had been difficult, but he was catching the hang of it now, and he was sure he had this one judged perfectly. Then he found himself rapidly approaching the line of trees. He took his eye off the ball to glance at the nearest tree, then looked back at the ball. It was dropping rapidly now and would not reach the trees. He held up, ran in a step, reached up, and hauled in the ball.

"Nice try!" he called. "You almost made it!"

"I shouldn't have tried," she said to him ruefully. "It only gave you a nice high one to grab."

"That was the idea!" he said, trotting past her.

As he reached down for the bat, he noticed a thin young man in a gray track suit. The man was walking toward them across the grass and seemed to have come from the direction of a low, light-colored brick building on the other side of the trees. The building looked like a school.

"Hello, there," the young man said, smiling. "I've

been watching you two fellows play ball. How come I haven't seen you around here sooner?"

"Aren't we supposed to play here?" Mike asked. He was disappointed. This was probably a private school playground, and they were trespassing.

"Nothing of the sort," the man assured him. His face was sharp and rawboned. From what he was wearing, it appeared that he probably did a lot of running. "I just wondered where you two came from, that's all. My name is Paul Franklin, and I coach a Little League team for this neighborhood. Seems to me we could use a couple of ball hawks like you. In fact, I know we could."

"Little League?"

"Sure. Are you boys new in town?"

Mike nodded. "We just moved in this week. My father got a new job. It was a big promotion, so he had to take it."

"Have you two ever played Little League before?"

"Just baseball, not Little League."

"How old are you?"

Jean had walked back in when Mike started talking to Paul Franklin, and now she was close enough to give her age. "I'm twelve. Mike's eleven."

"That's fine. Just the right age."

"For what?"

6

"Little League baseball."

"Hey!" Jean cried. "Hey, that would be great!"

"It sure would," agreed Mike. Then he added cautiously. "Could we *both* play?"

"Of course. Why not?"

Mike looked at Jean. As was usual whenever she played ball, she had done her hair in pigtails and tucked them up under her baseball cap. With the cap on and wearing her favorite, loose-fitting sweat shirt and jeans, she did indeed look like a boy.

Looking back at Paul Franklin, Mike grinned. "No reason," he said.

Jean spoke up then, a hint of suppressed merriment in her hazel eyes. "I'm Mike's sister, Mr. Franklin."

The man looked sharply at Jean, then lifted his head and laughed out loud. "Of course! I *thought* there was something about you . . . but you play so *well*. I mean, like a . . ."

"You mean like a boy?" Jean asked, obviously amused at the comparison.

"Well, yes," the man admitted, "like a boy."

"Where we used to live, Mr. Franklin," Mike explained, "there weren't always enough boys to make a team. Jean filled in all the time. She's *better* than most boys. You ought to see her pitch."

"Well, yes, I'm sure she must be very good."

7

"She's fast, and she's got a curve."

The man smiled and shook his head in wonder. "I guess during the baseball season it's a shame she *isn't* a boy."

"What do you mean by that, Mr. Franklin?" Jean asked, her voice sharp.

"Well, obviously, we can't include you on a Little League roster, Jean. And that's too bad, because as I said earlier, I really do need two more players."

"What positions do you need them for?"

"Outfield and third base."

"I could play third," said Jean.

"She's sure got the arm for it, Mr. Franklin," seconded Mike.

"I'm sure she has. But I'm afraid it's simply out of the question."

"Why, Mr. Franklin?" Jean asked.

"If she doesn't play," said Mike firmly, "I won't."

The man held up his hand quickly. His smile was apologetic. "Now let's not get all excited."

"Jean always played with us guys. None of us minded. She was a captain, usually. And you just saw how well she plays."

He smiled in agreement, then looked closely at Jean again. "You're right, Mike. Jean does know how to play ball—at least judging from what I saw."

Jean smiled. "Thank you, Mr. Franklin."

"So perhaps," Mr. Franklin went on, "we ought to forget for now that Jean's a girl and invite you both out tonight for a tryout. We'll let the rest of the team decide. How's that?"

Mike felt better at once. There was little doubt in his mind what the fellows would decide once they saw how well Jean played ball. And how well he played, too—hopefully.

"Sure, Mr. Franklin."

The man grinned. He seemed to like the idea the more he thought about it. "We haven't sent in for our Little League charter yet anyway—even though we play everything regulation Little League. But we will have to let the other guys decide."

"Fair enough," said Jean.

"Okay then," said Mr. Franklin. "This field around five. Can you make it?"

"We'll be there," said Mike.

As soon as Mr. Franklin started back through the trees in the direction from which he had come, Mike turned to Jean.

"Come on. Get out there. It's my turn to hit."

As soon as she was ready, he tossed the ball, stepped up and swung. He caught the ball just right, but his sister had been off at the crack of the bat. Mike held his breath as she raced toward the trees.

In front of a large maple, Jean spun around,

9

reached up, and gloved the ball—then threw it in with one quick motion. The ball took only one bounce before it slapped into his bare open palm.

It was a great catch, all right, Mike realized as he saw his sister start in—a big grin on her face—and those guys better not try to keep her off the team. But how could they?

She was almost as good a ballplayer as he was.

2

"WHAT'S THIS?" MIKE'S father asked, as he walked out onto the back porch and looked down at Mike and Jean. "Mother says you won't be eating supper with us this evening."

Mike was standing closest to his father; he and Jean were in the act of playing catch. He turned to look up at his father. "Jean and I are going to play Little League ball, Dad. We spoke to the coach this afternoon. Practice is at five. That's why we ate early."

Mike's father was a tall, square-shouldered man with cottonlike tufts of hair at his temples. His white shirt, as usual at this time of day, was open at the neck. Looking down at the two of them, he smiled. "I know. Your mother told me that, too. I was trying

11

to get a rise out of you." He looked over at Jean. "So you're going to be out there with the rest of the boys. That right, Jean?"

"Sure." She threw the ball back to Mike—hard. "I can play as well as any boy can." She grinned. "Except Mike, of course."

"Of course."

Mr. Tobin's square, relaxed face became momentarily set with concern, however, as a thought occurred to him. "Are you sure the rest of the boys aren't going to complain about playing with a girl? This isn't Sterling Valley, don't forget."

"I know *that,* all right," broke in Mike peevishly. "I only wish it were. We could just play ball then. But these guys better not say anything to me about Jean, that's all. Boy, I'd just like to hear them."

Jean laughed. "They won't say anything, Mike. And if they do, you just let me handle it."

"Okay. Okay," Mike said. "But they better not, just the same."

"Perhaps I shouldn't have brought the matter up," said Mike's father hastily. "I'm sure everything will go just fine tonight. I might take a walk over a little later to watch you practice."

"Oh, don't do that, Dad," said Jean. "You'll make me nervous."

"You won't make me nervous, Dad," said Mike.

12

"Well . . . I'll see."

Mr. Tobin turned and went inside the house. As the screen door slammed shut behind him, Jean called to Mike.

"Start throwing me grounders. Remember what Mr. Franklin said. He needs me at third."

"Okay. But I won't throw them right at you. You'll have to range to get them."

"Fine," Jean said, punching her glove. "Let's go."

Until a few minutes to five, Mike threw his sister ground balls, trying to keep them just out of her reach. But she surprised him time and again, coming up with them swiftly and surely and firing the ball across the yard to him with a snap and an accuracy he had not noticed in her throws before. She was good, he realized. Very good. And this renewed his determination to see that nothing at all be allowed to prevent her from playing ball. If his sister was not allowed to play, as he had told Mr. Franklin earlier, he would refuse to play as well, no matter how much they needed him.

Paul Franklin smiled when he saw the two of them approaching. He was dressed in light slacks, a T shirt,

13

and an old battered baseball cap was set back on his head. There was a thin fungo bat in his hand; and as Mike and Jean approached, he tossed a baseball into the air and hit a nice lazy fly to two boys waiting in the outfield. One of them broke for the ball, galloped in under it, reached up, and let the ball strike the heel of his glove. The ball went bouncing upon the ground ahead of him. The boy kept running, reached again for the ball, then booted it.

Mike smiled and turned to Jean. "These guys are clowns."

"Not so fast," cautioned Jean. "You can't say that for sure so soon."

Mike shrugged. "Maybe."

By this time they had reached Mr. Franklin. "You two are among the first to arrive. Fine." He looked at Jean. "I want you to keep those pigtails under your cap during this practice, Jean. We won't tell anyone anything at this time. We'll let your ability speak for itself."

"Fine," said Mike.

Mr. Franklin looked at Mike. "Did you say you were going to try out for outfield, Mike?"

Mike nodded. "That's where you said you needed help."

"Yes, I did. But I've been allowed two more fel-

14

lows in the player auction, and both of them claim to be outfielders."

Mike looked out at the two boys standing in the outfield near the trees. "You mean them?"

"Those are the boys."

"I have to beat them out?"

"To play regular. Yes."

Mike grinned at Mr. Franklin. "No problem," he said. "I'll go out there right now and show you."

Mr. Franklin laughed. "That's the spirit. You do that."

The boy who had just booted the fly ball nodded curtly to Mike as Mike trotted close. The other fellow said nothing and did not bother to nod. He was much taller than the other boy, and the look in his eyes and the cut of his chin caused Mike to pause momentarily as his glance swept over him. The boy looked as if he could really go get them—a ball hawk. The glove he was wearing was well oiled, battle worn, and had a deep pocket. Mike turned back around to wait for Mr. Franklin to hit another fly ball.

He didn't have long to wait. The coach's bat flashed around, and the ball went soaring high and far to Mike's left. Mike started after it. But he hadn't

15

taken more than a few quick strides before the tall boy swept easily past him, reached up almost nonchalantly, and hauled the ball down. Without breaking stride, he pegged the ball in to Mr. Franklin. The peg was low, long, and hard, bouncing only once before it slapped into Mr. Franklin's waiting palm.

The boy turned to Mike as soon as he pulled up and said, "Sorry, chum. That was my fly ball. You go next."

Mike nodded, punched his glove, and waited. All of a sudden he was not so certain that getting a berth on this team was going to be such a lead-pipe cinch.

Mr. Franklin sent another fly into the air, this time not so high or so far. Mike coasted over casually and reached up for the ball. To his surprise the ball slammed into his glove sooner than he had expected. Before he had time to clap his right hand over the ball to keep it in the pocket of his glove, the ball had popped out and was on its way to the ground. He grabbed for it, but missed.

When he finally did overtake the ball and throw it in, he remembered ruefully his remark about clowns to his sister—not too long before.

He kept his face averted from the other two boys as he trotted back to where they were waiting, but the taller one said quietly, "Take the next one, kid. This time put your glove up a little sooner."

Mike flushed angrily. He didn't need anyone to tell him how to catch a fly ball. But he said nothing, just nodded to the kid and punched his glove.

Mr. Franklin sent another ball skyward. This one was hit higher than any of the others, and as Mike broke for it, he realized he would have to come in quite a ways. He got on his horse and swept in under the ball and—remembering the tall fellow's remark—got his glove up a little sooner than he thought necessary. The ball steamed into his glove with a solid smack, and as Mike pulled it down and made his peg back in to Mr. Franklin, he realized how right that kid had been. Had he waited a moment longer to put up his glove, he would have booted the ball a second time.

As he trotted back out to the others, he watched the smaller of the two boys go after another fly ball, one hit to his left. The fellow charged in too far, then began to backpedal furiously. At the last moment he flung up his glove hand and just managed to spear the ball. The fellow had stuck with it, all right, but he was obviously having a terrible time judging fly balls.

As soon as the fellow threw the ball back, the taller one called something over to him. The small fellow nodded and pounded his glove nervously. Mike turned back around then in time for Mr. Franklin's next fly ball. The tall boy went after this one with smooth confidence, and as Mike watched him he noted how soon the boy's glove went up—well before the ball reached him. He pulled the ball down in one single fluid motion and threw in to Mr. Franklin.

It looked nice—the way it should look, Mike realized. Determined to look as well, he pounded his glove and leaned forward in expectation of Mr. Franklin's next fly.

But the man did not hit the ball. Instead, he tossed his bat aside and waved them in. Mike stood straight then, disappointed, and noticed how many other players had appeared on the field. There were many groups of them playing catch or standing around talking, and one complete contingent seemed to have arrived at once, each boy in a gray uniform with a blue stripe up the pants leg. They each wore a cap with a blue visor.

Mike wondered if they were going to play a game. His pulse quickening at the thought. He started to trot in.

"That's right," Mr. Franklin replied in answer to Mike's question. "That is the Hornet's team. They just got their uniforms, and they called me earlier to ask if we couldn't play a preseason scrimmage. I told their coach, sure thing."

Mike turned to Jean. "Hey, that's great. A game already."

Jean nodded, her eyes dancing at the prospect. "Do you think we'll get a chance to play?"

Mike turned back to the coach. "Does that mean we'll be able to play, Mr. Franklin?"

"Well . . . of course. I'll put in as many boys as I can." He smiled. "I want to get a look at all my prospects."

Mike and Jean left the coach then and walked over to a spot in back of first base where they could talk.

"Well," Mike began, "how'd you do? Anybody ask any questions?"

Jean shook her head and grinned impishly. "I worked out around third base while you were in the outfield, and I guess I did all right. The fellow who is going to play first base just threw grounders at us."

Mike nodded. "It'll be different in a real game, of course. That ball will be coming at you hot off the bat."

"I know, Mike. But I think I can handle it."

He grinned at her. "Just keep those pigtails under your cap."

She shrugged. "I feel kind of funny about that,

19

Mike. Some of the guys have been looking at me with a funny look in their eye. They're suspicious, I can tell. And I'd just as soon have them know I'm a girl. I really would."

"They'll know soon enough. After tonight's game for sure."

"I hope so, Mike."

"And boy, if they give you any static . . ."

"Please, Mike. No trouble. Besides, I don't think they will—not if I handle my position well enough, and maybe get some hits."

"Don't worry. You will."

She grinned. "Well, I *am* worried, Mike. So keep your fingers crossed."

"By the way, what's the name of our team?"

"The Dolphins."

Mike nodded. "I like that name."

Just then a boy Mike had not met before approached them, a wide grin on his face. He was tall and rawboned, his lanky wrists extending far out of his sleeves, and he was carrying a first baseman's glove.

"Here comes the first baseman," said Jean.

"Hey, you two," the boy said. "What are you trying to pull, anyway?"

Mike felt himself tighten all over. He frowned and

20

took a step forward to meet the boy. "What do you mean?"

The boy laughed out loud. It was a kind of hoot. But there was nothing mean in the laugh, and the boy's blue eyes were alive with mischief. "You know what I mean. Our new third baseman is a girl!"

Mike felt suddenly deflated. He didn't know what to say. He glanced quickly back at Jean, then at the boy. "So what's it to you?"

"Hey, I'm not complaining," the fellow protested amiably. "She looks just great around third. And what a whip she's got! But don't you think you should let the rest of the guys in on the secret?"

Jean smiled and shrugged. "How did you know?" she asked.

"By degrees," he said with a grin. "At first I thought you were kind of a sissy, the way you walked and all. But then when you started scooping up the baseballs I threw you and pegging them back to me as hard as you were doing, I didn't know what to think. So I was watching you over here talking to this guy . . ."

"This guy's my brother, Mike."

"Oh. Hi, Mike. I'm Steve Deforrest." He looked back at Jean. "Anyway, when I saw you talking to

21

your brother I saw you laugh—and all of a sudden I knew you were a girl."

"My name is Jean, Steve."

He grinned at her. "Hi."

"Are any of the others suspicious?" Mike asked.

"Sure. At least I think so."

Jean looked at Mike. "I think we should go and tell Mr. Franklin that the cat is out of the bag."

"May I come too?" Steve wanted to know. "I want to get credit for the discovery."

Jean laughed. "Sure. Come along."

As they walked over to where Mr. Franklin was talking to the coach of the other team, Mike's heart sank. He was certain the other coach would raise an objection to Jean's playing on the Dolphins. And even if he didn't, with everyone knowing she was a girl, how could his sister possibly get a fair trial?

3

WHEN THEY REACHED the coaches, it was Mike who spoke first. "We've got problems, Mr. Franklin."

The man smiled. "How's that, Mike?"

"I found out," spoke up Steve. "Jean's a girl."

Mr. Franklin did not seem surprised at Steve's announcement. He glanced at the coach standing beside him and then looked back at the three of them. "This is Pete Black," he told them. "He's the coach of the Hornets. Some of his players have already made the same discovery you did, Steve."

"Does that mean I can't play?" Jean asked.

"Not at all," said Pete Black, a bit of mischief in his eyes. "You'll just have to prove you can do the job at third base."

"What that means, I suspect," explained Mr.

Franklin to Jean, "is that Hornet batters are going to be trying to hit a lot of ground balls to the hot corner."

"Then it'll be a real test," said Steve.

"I should say so," said Mr. Franklin.

"I'm going to tell the other guys," said Steve. He turned and hurried away from them in the direction of a group of Dolphin players.

Jean sighed. "I don't know, Mr. Franklin," she said. "It gets to be more of a hassle every minute. I don't want to be causing all this trouble."

Mr. Black spoke up then. "Actually, Jean, I'm not sure Little League rules allow a girl to play on a Little League team. But so far we haven't received our charter. So as far as I can see, until we do—you have as much right as any boy to play for the Dolphins."

"As long as you pull your weight, Jean," Mr. Franklin added.

Jean nodded.

Mike was satisfied with that. He smiled at the coach. "Don't worry. She'll pull her weight, all right."

"Well, let's put that proposition to the test as of right now," the man said. He turned to Pete Black. "Are your boys all here?"

The coach nodded.

"Okay. You're the visitors. We'll take the field first. That suit you?"

"Fine."

Just before the coach of the Hornets turned to walk off, he paused and glanced at Jean. "Good luck, Jean."

She smiled at Mr. Black. "Thanks."

Mike was pleased to hear Mr. Franklin call his name out as the starting left fielder when the man read aloud the starting lineup. He was surprised, however, when it appeared that the tall outfielder Mike had shagged flies with earlier was not in the lineup also.

As he trotted out to his left field position, he was aware of his heart thumping in his throat—and also of just how swiftly things had changed for him during the course of this fabulous day.

That morning he had been really scraping bottom, so unhappy was he about their move to Addison. But from the moment Jean had knocked on his door until now, he had not thought once of Sterling Valley. Things had simply been happening too fast. And here he was starting in left field for the Dolphins—while his sister played third. Boy, if the guys in Sterling Valley could only see them now!

His thoughts were broken into by the sharp crack of a bat. Startled, Mike looked up in time to see the ball heading right for him. But he hadn't seen the ball strike the bat and didn't know whether to run in or stay where he was. Only when he saw how swiftly the ball was rising did he realize he had better get back —and fast.

He turned and raced back, his eyes never leaving the ball. Yet no matter how fast he ran, the ball continued to carry. When at last it began to fall, he reached his glove as high as he could. But the ball came down just inches beyond his outstretched glove, bounced once on the ground, then rolled all the way to the trees.

Even as he chased the ball into the trees, he knew it was hopeless. He could hear the other team cheering as the batter raced around the bases, and his own players yelling at him to throw the ball home. He picked up the ball finally, whirled, and fired. But even as he recovered from the throw, he saw the batter racing across the plate.

Pounding his glove ruefully, he came out from under the trees and took a deep breath. He should have had that fly ball, he realized. His hesitation in going back had turned a long fly into a home run.

Mike glanced in at the pitcher. The fellow was not yet back up on the mound, and he had his hands on his hips as he looked out at Mike.

Mike didn't look to the left or the right. All he could hope for now was another fly ball—one that he could put away neatly and quickly, to show these fellows that he wasn't as bad as that last hit made him look. But he just wasn't to be that fortunate, Mike realized, as the next three batters went out quietly— the first on a roller back to the pitcher, the second on a pop to second, and the third on a fast, one-hopper to third. Jean handled the ball flawlessly and threw the batter out by a full stride.

Mike trotted in, trying not to appear as depressed as he felt. As he sat down on the bench, Steve dropped down beside him and slapped him on the back. The first baseman's elfin face had a grin on it, as if he were selling peanut butter in a commercial.

"What's the matter out there, chum? You looked like you didn't want to go back for that one."

"I wasn't ready for it," Mike admitted ruefully. "I fell asleep."

"That's understandable," nodded Steve. "That guy hit the first pitch to him and really clocked it."

"I should have had it."

"Forget it. You'll get others."

"I hope."

Glancing down the bench, Mike saw Jean sitting quietly, talking to the pitcher. Beyond her, standing a little back of the bench, was the tall outfielder. Was the outfielder perhaps too old for Little League?

"Hey, who *is* that tall guy, anyway?" he asked Steve.

"The one standing behind the bench?"

Mike nodded.

"His name is Paul DiAngelo. He comes from across town. Coach says he enrolled too late in the player auction in his neighborhood, so he asked if he could play for us. It looked like we needed a player, so the coach said okay."

"How old is he?"

"Beats me. But he sure looks older than twelve, but he's probably just big for his age."

"Hey, Steve! Come on!"

Both boys swung around quickly to see the coach standing in front of the on-deck circle with a bat in his hand. The lead-off batter had just tossed his bat aside and was in the process of walking down to first.

Steve hustled out to the on-deck circle, grabbed the bat the coach handed him, hefted it a couple of times, and then went down on one knee as the second batter walked around behind the catcher and got himself set in the batter's box.

Everyone was calling to the batter, "Come on, Lee!" Mike took up the shout as well. On the second pitch, Lee swung and sent a line drive over short. The Hornet center fielder crossed over to cut it off, put his glove down, and missed the ball. Still traveling with great speed, the ball scooted across the grass while the left fielder and the center fielder raced after it.

Lee rounded second going full out, and Coach Franklin waved him around third. The throw-in to the plate was a full stride behind the flying heels of the batter. Mike joined the rest of the team in congratulating Lee; his home run had wiped out the Hornet lead with one stroke, and now they were ahead!

As Mike sat back down, he felt as if a burden had been lifted from his shoulders. He had blamed himself entirely for that one-run lead of the Hornets. Now he could forget it—almost.

The next three batters hit the ball well in each case, but right at somebody. Mike found himself trotting back out to his position, hoping for some fly balls to left. He wanted to show what he could do when he wasn't asleep.

The first batter up for the Hornets smashed a line drive right at second. The second baseman knocked it down, then threw out the runner. Steve made a nice stretch to flag down the throw.

The next batter singled over second base, and Lee swooped in from center field to scoop up the ball and send it back into the infield. The base runner rounded first, then trotted back to the bag.

One man on, one out.

The next batter fouled off two straight pitches, then swung on a wide pitch and missed. Mike punched his glove. Good. Two outs.

The batter getting set at the plate didn't look like much of a stickman. He was small and wiry, and he batted from a curious crouch, his head leaning out over the plate. He watched the first pitch go by for a called strike one, then straightened suddenly on the next pitch as he swung from his heels and connected solidly.

Mike was off at the crack of the bat—as the ball left the bat on a line into left field. The ball rose to a height just above the line of trees behind the park and went no higher. As Mike raced in, he realized he had a decision to make—whether to catch the ball on one hop for a single, in which case there would be batters on first and third, or catch it on the fly to end the inning.

He decided he would end the inning.

Racing in at full tilt, he reached out for the ball. But it was sinking now more rapidly than he had realized. Mike ran still harder, aware that he had committed himself now and could not pull up in time to field the ball on a bounce. As he saw how low the ball was, he dived for it desperately.

It was a fine effort. The ball struck the thumb of his glove, then shot off at an angle past him. As Mike sprawled forward onto the grass, he caught himself quickly, rolled over, and jumped to his feet to race after the ball. But Lee Wagner had been backing him up, and it was he who reached the ball first and made the throw back to the infield.

Lee's peg was a good one. The second baseman almost caught the batter off second, but the runner reached back and grabbed the sack before the tag was made.

But the tying run had scored.

The next batter up struck out to end the inning.

"Too bad, kid," said Paul DiAngelo as Mike neared the bench. "You almost pulled it off."

"I should have played it for a single."

The tall kid shrugged. "Maybe."

Mr. Franklin came over then and slapped Mike

warmly on the back. "Nice try, Mike. It's early in the game yet. We'll get that run back."

"I sure hope so."

"Just don't let that play get you down. I'd rather see a ballplayer take a few chances once in a while than play everything safe."

That made Mike feel a little better. But as he sat down on the bench and reviewed his performance in the field so far in the game, he was not at all encouraged. He had two chances and had let a run score each time without getting the out.

And Paul DiAngelo was still standing in back of the bench—waiting.

Bob Corbett, the catcher, was up. He was a round, cheerful kid with a mess of freckles on his nose and cheeks. At the moment, however, there was a very determined frown on his face as he swung his bat in anticipation of the first pitch. The Hornet pitcher unwound and let the ball go. It was a fast pitch, and the ball wasted no time at all getting to the plate. But Bob Corbett swung just as fast.

Catching the ball on the fat end of his bat, Bob sent a scorching line drive through the infield, between short and third. He was puffing a little when he reached first, but there was a pleased grin on his face.

And that brought up Jean.

Steve was sitting beside Mike on the bench. Now he nudged Mike in the side. "Okay, Mike, here we go. Get into the on-deck circle. You're up after your sister."

As Mike grabbed a bat and headed for the on-deck circle, he moistened suddenly dry lips—and wondered a little desperately if he was nervous for himself or for Jean. He was worried about both, he realized as he went down on one knee in the on-deck circle and watched his sister hitch her jeans up a bit around her waist and take her position in the batter's box.

Her first practice swing made him think that he really might have reason for worrying. But he shoved the thought quickly out of his mind. She could *hit* as well as anyone—no matter how she swung.

The first pitch to her was inside, and she let it go for a ball. The next pitch was over the plate, and she swung, fouling the ball off to the right.

"You can hit it, Jean!" Steve shouted from the bench behind Mike.

Jean stepped out of the batter's box, reached down for a handful of dirt, which she quickly rubbed into the palms of her hands, then adjusted her cap. Stepping back into the batter's box, Mike heard the Hornet catcher say something to her. He didn't catch the words, but saw Jean blush. He compressed his lips and looked away. He couldn't afford to get into any kind of scrape with this guy now, but later . . . after the game . . .

The solid crack of a bat brought Mike's attention back to the game. He swung his eyes up in time to see the ball Jean had just hit sail lazily over the second baseman's lunging glove and drop in for a base hit. The bench behind Mike erupted with cheers as Jean crossed first and Bob Corbett raced all the way around to third, where he pulled up puffing like a steam engine.

Mike got to his feet. Now it was his turn. Jean had shown what she could do. Could he do as well? He had better, he suddenly realized.

The first pitch to him was low, and he didn't offer at it. The fellow umpiring called it a strike. Mike didn't argue. He took a deep breath and waited for the next pitch. This time the pitch looked as if it were coming right over the plate. Mike swung and missed. The catcher held up the ball for Mike to see, then pegged it back to his pitcher. Mike stepped out of the batter's box to get some dirt on his palms. They were so sweaty it was difficult for him to get a firm grip on the handle of his bat.

Stepping back in, he heard Steve and other members of the Dolphins yelling encouragement to him. The pitcher went into his windup and fired the ball. It came faster than the previous pitch, and this one also looked like it was right down the pipe. Mike swung—and missed. The yells from the bench abruptly ceased as Mike stepped out of the batter's box and lugged his useless bat back to the bat rack.

"That's too bad," Steve said. "But don't take it to heart. It looks like this pitcher is throwing aspirin tablets."

"Well, he's fast," replied Mike gloomily. "That's for sure."

The next batter was Paul Swenson. He swung on the second pitch and sent a dribbler to the second baseman. The infielder got his glove on the ball, dropped it, picked it up, and then dropped it again. By the time he found the handle, the Dolphin pitcher was across first base, Bob Corbett had scored, and Jean was on third.

Billy Cashman, the right fielder, singled up the middle next, scoring Jean. But he died on first as Lee Wagner and Steve struck out to end the inning.

"I was right," said Steve, as he returned to the bench for his glove. "That guy *is* throwing aspirin tablets after all."

Mike grinned at him. "Well, don't take it to heart."

"Mike!"

Mike turned to see the coach and Paul DiAngelo hurrying toward him. His heart sank. He knew even before the coach spoke what the man was about to say.

"I'm putting Paul in now, Mike," the coach said, as soon as he reached Mike.

Mike nodded. "Sure, Coach."

Mr. Franklin turned to Paul DiAngelo. "Take center field, Paul. Just tell Lee to move over into left field."

Paul nodded and trotted quickly out onto the field. Mike watched the boy go, then turned to look at the coach. "I guess that means you don't think you'll be needing me. Is that right, Mr. Franklin?"

"No, it isn't, Mike. You'll get plenty of chances to play for the Dolphins this season. But this fellow DiAngelo comes very highly recommended, and I liked what I saw earlier. I'm sure he can help the team. And that's really the important thing, Mike. Isn't it?"

"Sure, Mr. Franklin."

Mike left the man then and went back to the bench, sitting down next to the other outfielder Mike had shagged flies with before the game. But the boy said nothing to Mike. He just stared straight ahead, listlessly punching his glove—obviously a very unhappy young man who had just about given up already.

And that didn't make Mike feel any better, especially when he looked out onto the field and saw his sister playing third while he rode the bench.

He hated to admit it to himself, but he was actually embarrassed.

4

FROM THAT INNING ON Paul Swenson began to show the Hornet batters just as much speed as the Hornet pitcher had been showing them as he proceeded to blow the ball past the batters. The result was that four innings later, the score was still four to two in favor of the Dolphins, with the Hornets batting in the top of the sixth.

This was it, Mike realized, as he leaned forward on the bench—his disappointment at being pulled from the lineup overcome now by his desire to see the Dolphins win this ball game.

The first Hornet batter of the inning stepped into the batter's box, and Mike saw him flick a quick look down to third. *He's going to try to get one past Jean,* he thought.

On the first pitch the batter swung around and bunted the ball down the third-base line. He was not trying to get it past Jean—just catch her sitting back on her heels. But Jean was on her way down the line as soon as the batter swung around to bunt. Now, still racing in at full tilt, she reached down with her bare hand, caught the ball cleanly, and fired over to first.

But the throw was high and wild. Steve made a great jump to save the ball from sailing into the trees behind the stands. It was a fine effort on his part, but the runner was safe; and at once the Hornet bench began to ride Jean.

"She's blowing up!" someone cried.

"There she goes!" answered another.

As the next Hornet batter stepped up to the plate, two or three of his teammates yelled at him to hit the ball to third for a sure hit.

Mike seethed inwardly and hung on to the bench with both hands. But he didn't say anything back to them. If he were on third, he realized, he wouldn't want his sister yelling back at those who might be riding him.

The Hornet batter made as if to bunt, but didn't.

"Strike!" the umpire cried.

The batter stepped out and rubbed some dirt on the handle of his bat. Then he pulled his helmet down securely, looked straight at Jean, and got back into the batter's box.

"Here it comes, Pigtails!" someone on the Hornet bench yelled.

The batter swung hard on Swenson's second pitch —and missed by an embarrassing margin.

Mike couldn't contain his glee. "*Thattaway* to pitch in there, Paul!" he yelled.

The batter dug himself a good toehold and readied himself for the next pitch. Paul Swenson fired a fast one right down the pipe. The batter uncoiled and caught the ball on the handle of his bat, sending a towering pop fly that drifted back into foul territory in back of third base.

The catcher threw his mask aside and raced for the ball, his face skyward. But Jean was going for it, too, and she was closest. As she raced past the Hornet bench for the ball, every player got to his feet and razzed her.

"You're going to miss it! You're going to miss it!"

"Watch out for the stands!"

"It's too far! It's too far!"

But Jean kept after it, reached up, and caught the ball while still running at full speed from third base. She whirled quickly after catching the ball and fired to Al Dekin on second. Al seemed a little surprised, and then he smiled broadly, realizing why Jean had thrown it to him so hard. After a foul fly, the runner can advance if he tags up. The Hornet runner on first had forgotten that as had his first base coach . . . but Jean hadn't.

Heads up ball, that's real heads up ball, Mike commented to himself happily.

The next Hornet batter didn't seem to be so anxious to take advantage of the fact that Jean was playing third. He swung away on Swenson's first good pitch and spanked a single into center, sending the runner on first to third and pulling up on first himself.

Mike frowned. Now the tying run was on first and the go-ahead run at the bat. As the next Hornet batter stepped in, it seemed to Mike that the batter was well aware of how important his role in this game had suddenly become. He seemed quite nervous, wiggling his bat all the while he waited for the pitch.

Paul Swenson pitched. The batter lost his nervousness at once, it seemed, and swung hard, connecting solidly. Mike jumped to his feet. The ball was bounding swiftly down the third-base line, right at Jean. She came in a step, snaring the ball cleanly about chest high. Instead of throwing home, Jean threw over to second to start what she hoped would be a game-ending double play.

But for the second time that evening her throw was a little high. This time it was Al Dekin who had to jump to get the ball; and though he was able to tag the bag a step ahead of the runner for the force out, his throw to first was not in time to catch the batter —and one more run had scored to make it Dolphins four, Hornets three, with the tying run on first.

Mike was upset. Should Jean have thrown home? Still, there were two outs. Only one more to go and they'd have it all wrapped up.

"You blew it!" someone on the Hornet bench screeched. "You should have thrown home!"

Mike saw Jean look at the bench for just an instant and realized the moment she did that it was a mistake. And sure enough, the entire Hornet bench opened up on her, and Mike had all he could do to keep his mouth shut.

Mr. Franklin came over, patted Mike quietly on the shoulder, and then moved off without a word. The coach understood, it seemed.

The next batter fouled off Swenson's first pitch, then tied into his next one, sending a towering fly to Billy Cashman in right field. Billy stood still for a long moment, then abruptly started to backpedal. But he was not fast enough, and the misjudged fly ball dropped beyond him.

With two outs the runner on first had been flying

since the moment the ball left the batter's bat. Mike glanced at him and saw that he was already close to third, and the third base coach was waving him in. But Paul DiAngelo had raced over to back Billy Cashman up. With scarcely a break in stride, he reached down, fielded the ball Billy had missed, and fired home.

It was a great throw, low and hard—a long clothes-line. Bob Corbett planted himself in front of the plate as the Hornet runner pounded around third and headed toward him. The ball bounced once just beyond the pitcher's mound. Bob caught the ball in his glove, then bent forward to tag the sliding runner. In the explosion of dust that followed, the only thing that mattered to Mike was the umpire's right thumb as he hooked it over his shoulder.

The runner was out!

It took a while for the pandemonium to settle down enough for the Dolphins to shake hands with the Hornets in recognition of a tight, well-played ball game. As the coach of the other team said to Coach Franklin, "If this is what it is going to be like in regular season play, we're all going to have gray hairs."

Mike saw Mr. Franklin laugh in agreement to that

43

comment, and then he turned to Mike. "Your sister did all right, Mike. Now let's find out what the rest of the team thinks."

As soon as the Dolphins and their coach had moved off, Mr. Franklin called all of the team members together. When they had gathered in a circle around him, he spoke. "I told Jean and Mike that we would let the rest of you decide after our game if you wanted Jean to play or not." He looked quickly around the tense circle of faces. "But before we take a vote, I'd like you all to feel that you are free to speak your mind about this." He turned then and looked squarely at Jean. "I'm sure Jean won't mind—not after what she had to put up with from that Hornet bench."

"Go ahead," said Jean, nodding vigorously. "I can take it."

"Why don't you move off, Jean," suggested Paul DiAngelo. "We don't want to hurt your feelings."

"So who's going to hurt her feelings?" protested Mike at once.

"See what I mean?" said Paul.

"Go ahead," said Jean. "Speak your mind."

"All right, I will. I don't think you should go on with this business of trying to be a boy—since you're obviously a girl."

Jean laughed. "If that's an insult, I didn't mind. But who said I was trying to be a boy?"

"Well, aren't you?"

"No. I'm trying to be a third baseman."

"And she didn't do so badly, at that," said Steve Deforrest.

"Seems to me you had a little difficulty with one of her throws," retorted Paul.

"Now, hold it, fellows," said the coach. "Let's keep this friendly."

"Look," insisted Paul, "all I'm saying is that it's crazy for a girl to play baseball. She's not supposed to play baseball. How many major league baseball players are there who are women, anyway?"

"None," admitted Jean. "But what does that prove?"

"Oh, I see. You're going to be the first one."

Jean tossed her head. "I have no intention of playing ball in the major leagues."

"Well, that proves it, then."

"What do you mean by that?" Bob Corbett asked.

"Don't you see? Don't any of you guys see what I mean? My uncle played for Detroit a few years back. I used to watch him on television. And someday I want to play in the majors, and maybe some of you guys will be trying to make it there, too. And that's why many of us play Little League baseball, to prepare us for the big time. But Jean says she has no intention of playing in any major league—so what's she doing here playing ball with us?"

There was a general murmur of appreciation for that point of view, and Jean shrugged in resignation as she looked around at the rest of the players. But Mr. Franklin cleared his throat to get everyone's attention.

"Listen, fellows," he said, "Little League ball should help you all to be better ballplayers, and if some of you want to build on this experience and become major leaguers some day, that's fine. But that's not the only reason for playing Little League ball. If it were, I wouldn't want to coach it. The headaches wouldn't be worth it."

"Then why *do* we play Little League ball, then?" Paul demanded.

"It's very simple," the coach replied with a broad grin. "To have fun. That's right. To have a good time with your friends. To play a game you all like and to learn to win and lose with dignity. That's what life is all about, boys. And I happen to think that is something girls should learn about too."

"*Fun?*"

The coach laughed outright. "Of course! To have

fun! What's so strange about that?" He looked around at the rest of them. "Tell me, fellows, did you have any fun tonight?"

The response was loud and to the point. Everyone agreed. They had indeed had a good time.

"Sure," protested Paul doggedly, "but that's because we won."

"That's right. And we'll win some more and have more fun. And we'll lose some, too. But we'll have a good time in those games if we always play as well as we know how."

Paul was upset. "You're dodging the issue. Girls don't belong in baseball. It's a man's game. She'll get hurt."

Coach Franklin glanced at Jean. "He's right, you know. You could get hurt, as could any player."

Jean shrugged. "I don't care."

"Oh, boy," said Paul. "That's quite an attitude."

"Well, thank you, Paul," said the coach, "for speaking out so frankly. I think we all understand how you feel now." He turned from Paul then and looked around at the others. "Is there anyone else who wants to say something."

"What do you think, Coach?" Lee Wagner asked.

The coach considered a moment before replying. Then he said, "I spent some time this afternoon with myself trying to think of a good logical reason why Jean shouldn't play on our team. And the only one I could come up with was if she wasn't a good enough ballplayer, she shouldn't play."

"So that's what we have to decide," said Steve. "Is she a good enough ballplayer for the Dolphins."

"And that," said Coach Franklin, "is what we should now vote on. It's getting late."

Every boy nodded.

"All those who think Jean should be on our roster," said Coach Franklin, "raise your hand."

Every player, save two, put up their hand. The two were Paul DiAngelo and Skip Wiesmann. Mike thought he understood at once why Skip didn't want Jean on the team—it would make it almost impossible for him to play now, since he just wasn't that good a player.

So where does that leave you? he thought ironically. But he thrust the question from his mind, especially when he saw the sudden smile on his sister's face.

She'd made it! His sister was now a full-fledged member of the Dolphins!

5

"Well, of course, I'll be on hand to watch the opener," said Mike's father with a grin. "You can't expect me to stay home at a moment like this!"

The Tobin family was in the backyard, the charcoal already beginning to glow in the barbecue cooker. It was the first really warm evening of the spring, and it felt like summer already.

"And I'm coming too," said Mrs. Tobin, as she came out the back door, carrying a platter of buns and hamburgers. "After all, Babe Didrikson was a woman I admired very much."

"Babe Didrikson? Who was that?" asked Mike.

"Babe Didrikson Zaharias," replied Mike's father as he began to place hamburger patties on the grate over the fire. "She was a very fine woman athlete."

"Oh," said Mike.

"Sure. I have heard of her," said Jean.

Her mother smiled. "I heard she worked out with the Brooklyn Dodgers once, but I don't believe a girl has ever played in the majors."

"Yeah," said Mike. "That's what that creep, Paul DiAngelo said."

Mrs. Tobin was placing paper plates on the picnic bench. She looked at Mike. "Who's Paul DiAngelo?"

"He's a kid on the team."

"A very good player," said Jean. "He's probably going to make baseball a career. At least, he seems that serious about it."

"That's right. He's all business."

"He had a few things to say the night the team decided to let me play."

"He was against it," said his father. "Right?"

Jean nodded soberly. "His point was that if I wasn't going to play in the majors someday, what was the use of my playing now. Little League ball is supposed to be just a preparation for the majors."

Her father smiled at that. "I see what you mean. This Paul DiAngelo really must be all business. No time for fun."

Jean nodded. Her father turned his attention back to the spattering hamburger meat. Mike walked over to the table and sat down. It occurred to him that all the talk was about Jean playing on the Dolphins. After all, *he* was going to play tonight as well. Mr. Franklin had told him that at practice the day before. He was going to let Billy Cashman pitch, since he had pitched quite a bit last year according to what he had told the coach, and Paul Swenson would not be able to make the game until later in the evening. That would give Mike a chance to start in right field, and Mike accepted gladly. The thought of Jean starting while he sat on the bench had not been a pleasant one.

"Jean," said her mother, "how about putting that baseball glove down for a minute and helping me bring out the lemonade and coffee?"

Jean tossed her glove on the grass and followed her mother up the back porch steps.

Mike's father glanced at Mike. "What position did you say you'll be playing, Mike?"

"Right field."

He nodded, satisfied. "So what do you think of this town now?"

"Well, ever since I started playing ball with the Dolphins, it hasn't seemed so bad."

He smiled, obviously relieved. "That's fine, Mike. I'm glad to hear that. You were pretty upset about our move away from Sterling Valley, I noticed."

Mike was surprised. He hadn't realized that his father had noticed how upset he had been—and how concerned it had made him. But he could tell now from the smile of relief that had flooded his face that his father had been concerned.

"Get a few hits for the Tobins tonight, Mike."

"I sure will, Dad."

As Jean and his mother pushed their way out of the kitchen with the jugs of lemonade and iced coffee, Mike relaxed. Maybe all the talk *was* about Jean playing for the Dolphins, but his father knew he was playing too—and he guessed, somewhat ruefully, that he should have realized this all along.

Pleasantly aware of the feel of the new uniform he was wearing for the first time, Mike trotted into the outfield as the game got underway. The first Giant batter looked tall enough, so he moved back a ways and waited for Billy Cashman's first pitch.

It was in the dirt, but Bob Corbett managed to dig it out and fire it back to Billy without delay. The next pitch was over the plate, and the batter swung on it. He caught the ball late and sent a lazy fly into short right field.

Mike had backed out quite far, and he realized at

once that he would have to really dig to catch this one on the fly. Even as he raced in, he could see Paul DiAngelo racing over from center and cutting in behind him to back him up in case he missed it. Mike raced in even harder, his eye on the ball every second. It was falling now, but Mike was pretty sure by this time that he was going to be able to reach it.

At the last possible moment he reached out with his glove and felt the ball smack warmly into its pocket. He pulled up, enormously relieved, and threw the ball back in to Al Dekin at second.

As he trotted back to his position, Paul called over to him. "Nice run, Mike. Very pretty. That's the way to go get 'em."

Mike thanked him with a wave. He felt great and was just as pleased himself at the catch, but he wondered if perhaps he was playing out a little too deep. Mike edged in closer as the next batter stepped into the batter's box. He was a small, chunky fellow who liked to lean over the plate as he waited for the pitch.

Billy sent him two wild pitches in a row, both of which caused the batter to jump out of the batter's box. Billy fussed around on the mound to settle down, then came in with a pitch that wasn't wild. It was over the plate, and the batter swung, sending a low line drive over second for a clean single.

Paul pounced on the ball as soon as it reached him and fired the ball in to second.

"One out!" he called. "One out, guys! Let's get two this time!"

Mike grinned over at Paul. He was some spark plug, all right, probably just what the team needed.

But the next batter sent another line shot through the infield to put runners on first and third with only one out.

Mike punched his glove and edged in. It didn't look to him as if Billy Cashman was as good a pitcher as Swenson. He became even more certain of this when Billy, obviously unwilling to give the Giant batters anything good to hit, walked the next batter to load the bases.

"Play at any base!" yelled Paul from center field.

Mike punched his glove. *That's right,* he thought. *If they can do it.*

With the sacks crowded, Billy Cashman pitched as carefully as he could and got two quick strikes on the next batter, who had obviously been looking for a walk. Mike watched the Giant batter dig in and pounded his glove. Billy pitched. The batter swung, and the sound of the crack as bat met ball resounded throughout the little park. It was a clean hit, and the ball started to rise.

At once, Mike saw that it was to him. He started

back. But the ball kept rising. He raced back harder and realized as he ran that he had allowed himself to edge too far in. He took his eye off the ball in order to run harder, looked back, and saw the ball dropping just beyond him. He reached out for it. The ball caught the outstretched fingers of his glove, then glanced off. As he tried to overtake it, he saw Paul swoop over, field the ball, and throw the ball in.

Pulling up, Mike turned and saw that the throw was a great one, holding the batter to a triple. It was Jean who fielded the throw and almost caught the base runner off the bag.

But three runs had scored—on a fly ball Mike was convinced he could have caught easily if he had been positioned for it better.

"Play back a little more, Mike," called Paul as he trotted back to his position.

All Mike could do was nod to that. He felt no resentment that Paul should feel he could give him advice, not when Paul showed on almost every play what an alert ballplayer he was. Mike pounded his glove miserably. They were three runs down, and it was all his fault.

The next batter lined a shot right back at Billy Cashman, and the one after that struck out on one of Billy's wildest pitches.

"Hey, he's settling down," grinned Paul, as he trotted in beside Mike.

"Yeah. But we're already three runs down."

"Don't worry. We'll get those runs back. We've got plenty of time."

But Mike was not so sure of that a few minutes later. As the lead-off batter for the Dolphins, he had struck out on a wide, sweeping curve ball that had almost got past the catcher. Then Lee Wagner grounded out feebly to first, and Steve Deforrest struck out on a fast ball that had him shaking his head in disbelief as he trotted over to the bench for his glove.

Now, trotting back out to his position in right beside Paul, he remarked: "Looks like this guy pitching for the Giants really has something."

"Now, look, Mike. All he's got is a ball with laces on it, like any other baseball. He puts his pants on one leg at a time, like anyone else, and he only uses one arm to pitch with. Relax. We'll get to him."

Mike smiled. Paul's confidence was infectious. He pounded his glove with enthusiasm as he turned about to face the infield. Paul was right. The game wasn't over yet.

Billy Cashman started off by striking out the first two batters that faced him. Mike called over to Paul, "Hey! Looks like he *has* settled down."

"Stay loose, just in case," Paul called back to him.

Two pitches later Billy served up a fat one, and the Giant batter slashed it back through the box for a single. Obviously upset by this, Billy walked the next batter to put runners on first and second.

Mike punched his glove and leaned forward as the next batter—a lefty—strode up to the plate.

"Lefty!" Paul called to Mike. "Move over!"

But Mike was already on his way. A few paces from the foul line, he pulled up as Billy's first pitch came in high for a ball. Mike shifted his feet nervously, while Billy Cashman stomped about the mound. Then Billy tugged at the beak of his cap, leaned in for the sign, and went into his windup. It was a fast ball he sent toward the plate, and the batter was waiting for it. He uncoiled and swept his bat around, catching the ball just right.

But Mike had positioned himself perfectly. He watched the ball rise into the air, trotted back a few steps, turned, and waited. The ball dropped; Mike reached up and caught it for the third out.

As he trotted in beside Paul, the center fielder said, "Nice catch. You went back on that one just fine."

"Thanks," said Mike. "Now, if we can just get some runs."

Pete Ceballos was obviously thinking the same thing. He strode aggressively into the first pitch sent his way and spanked a clean single into center field. Paul DiAngelo left the on-deck circle, discarded two of the three bats he had been wielding, and strode to the plate.

"Get a hold of one!" called Mike.

A few other players yelled encouragement as Paul got himself set at the plate; and as Mike watched him, he got the feeling that Paul really knew what he was doing. He seemed perfectly at home at the plate.

And that was not the way he had felt, Mike remembered, as he recalled how it had been for him as lead-off batter the previous inning. He shook off the thought.

Paul took the first pitch inside, staying calmly inside the batter's box as the ball seemed to brush his shirt front. The next pitch was outside, and again the center fielder refused to offer at it. The Giant pitcher took off his cap and wiped perspiration off his forehead with the back of his hand. Paul waited, bat poised, eyes on the pitcher—as silent and ready as a

cat ready to pounce. The pitcher glanced at the runner on first, went into his stretch, and fired the ball
plateward.

Paul swung—on a level and following through perfectly, smashing the ball on a line into right center.
Mike jumped to his feet and watched as the ball
struck the turf once, almost precisely between the
center and right fielders, and hopped swiftly past
them. Only the fact that it hit one of the trees and
bounced sharply back prevented Paul from getting
more than two bases; but when he pulled up on second, Pete Ceballos had already scored standing up.

"Keep it going!" cried Mr. Franklin. "Everybody
hits!"

And it looked that way when Al Dekin poled a
long one into left center for a triple, sending Paul
home with the second run.

But Bob Corbett got tied up on an inside pitch and
sent a towering pop fly into the air over the home
plate. The Giant catcher staggered around under it
for what seemed like a full minute—then put the cap
on it for the first out.

And that brought up Jean.

Up until that moment the Giant bench had been
relatively quiet as had the players in the field. But at
sight of Jean approaching the plate, a few shrill whis-

tles came from the bench, and the Giant infield began advising Jean on various matters.

"Don't let your hair get in the way!"

"Hey, you're going to trip on your skirts going down to first!"

How many skirts is she supposed to be wearing? Mike was angry. *Besides, she's not wearing skirts. She's wearing a uniform like the rest of us.*

But the comments kept coming as Jean watched the first pitch to her cross the plate for a called strike.

"Don't be frightened," the Giant shortstop yelled. "Just close your eyes and swing!"

But the advice stopped suddenly as Jean swung on a high outside pitch and sent a soft liner into right field. As she hustled down the first base line, every player on the Dolphins jumped to his feet and cheered wildly. Al Dekin scored easily from third, and as he reached the plate, he jumped on it with both feet, a wide grin on his face.

In all the excitement Billy Cashman almost forgot that he was the next batter. But after he took the first pitch for a strike, things settled down somewhat. Mike watched him from the on-deck circle and felt a tightening of apprehension. Suppose he didn't get a hit, even though Jean, his own sister, had?

Billy Cashman swung on a low pitch and missed

for strike two. Mike swung the two bats he held around his head a couple of times, then watched the Giant pitcher unwind. The pitch came fast, and Billy swung just a little too late.

Two outs.

Mike got up and journeyed to the plate. He felt that all eyes were on him and that—like him—everyone was wondering if he could hit as well as his sister. As he dug in at the plate, the catcher grinned at him through his mask.

"What are you, the kid brother?"

Mike took a practice swing without replying to the catcher.

"Well, you'd better get a hit," continued the catcher, "or you'll never hear the end of it. You'll be the one doing the dishes from then on." The fellow grinned maliciously as he realized he had struck a vulnerable chord.

Mike compressed his lips grimly and waited for the first pitch. The pitcher unwound and let the ball go. It seemed to Mike that the ball was way inside. He hastened to pull himself out of the path of the ball, and then watched in dismay as the ball cut lazily away from him and sliced over the heart of the plate.

"Strike one!" cried the umpire.

Mike looked back at the man, then glanced at the

Dolphin bench. The players were all watching him nervously, as if they fully expected him to strike out.

Only Paul DiAngelo's voice broke the silence. "Straighten one out, Mike! You can do it!"

And then from first, Jean cried, "Get a hold of one, Mike!"

Mike stepped back into the batter's box.

"Feel that tension," said the Giant catcher. "Isn't it awful?"

Mike's mouth went dry. This catcher had a real talent for getting under his skin, Mike realized. Never before in his life had he been needled so expertly.

And then—almost before he was ready—Mike saw the next pitch roaring in on him. He tried to pull himself together in time to swing, but the ball smacked into the catcher's mitt before Mike could even get the bat around.

Strike two.

Mike's heart sank. He would have to hit this next pitch. He couldn't let this one go by.

"Watch out for this next pitch," the catcher told Mike. "It's coming right for your head—a waste pitch!"

But Mike wasn't listening any longer. Even though he could see that the ball was inside, he brought his bat around swiftly and caught the ball on the handle of his bat. He followed through as best he could and started to dig for first; but he was no more than a halfway down the first base line before the pitcher fielded his weakly hit grounder, straightened, and threw him out.

Three outs. The inning was over. But at least the Dolphins had tied the score.

Mike had no chances in the field the next inning; and when he trotted in toward the bench, he saw that Swenson had arrived finally. He looked fresh and eager to play in his new Dolphin uniform—sparkling white with red stripes down the pants, red sox, and a red visor on the cap. It reminded Mike at once of how he must look, and how anxious he was to stay on this team.

Lee Wagner struck out on a fast ball, and then Steve Deforrest singled through the middle. A moment later it became a rally as Pete Ceballos singled and Paul DiAngelo walked to load the bases. The excitement faded, however, when Al Dekin struck out and Bob Corbett sent a high fly to center field, which the Giant center fielder gathered in quickly and smoothly.

Mike grabbed his glove and started for the outfield.

63

But before he'd taken a couple of strides, he heard Coach Franklin calling his name. He turned.

The coach was standing with Paul Swenson and Billy Cashman, and as soon as Mike stopped and turned to face them, Billy started to trot out toward right field and Swenson began to walk out to the mound.

"I'm putting in Paul Swenson, Mike," the coach called out to him. "And Billy will be playing right field."

Mike nodded, glanced quickly into the stands to see if his mother and father were there, and then walked back to the suddenly very empty bench. The only other player sitting there with him was Skip Wiesmann. He looked at Skip. Skip looked at him.

Mike took a deep breath and turned his head to watch the game—but his heart wasn't in it; and though he tried not to admit it, he felt a smoldering resentment every time he caught sight of Jean fielding the easy rollers Steve was throwing her.

Mr. Franklin stopped by Mike. "Just want to get a good look at everyone this game, Mike," he explained.

Mike compressed his lips and nodded. "Sure, Mr. Franklin," he said.

Mike wanted to believe the coach, but he found it

difficult to believe the man would be putting in players just so he could look them over in a tight, three-to-three ball game. Still . . . maybe Mike was wrong.

Yet no matter how hard he tried to shake that earlier feeling of resentment, it only grew in intensity as the game went on.

6

THERE WAS AT LEAST ten minutes left in the lunch period. Mike was at the end of one of the tables in the cafeteria working diligently at his math assignment, hoping he could get it done before the end of the lunch period so he wouldn't have to take the work home.

His forehead resting on his left palm, he was so completely lost in his computations that at first Mike did not realize that his name had been mentioned. When he did realize it, he looked up, startled. Four or five faces were turned toward him, open laughter on some, amusement on others—every kid at the table next to him, it seemed, having good laughs at his expense.

"We were just talking about baseball, Mike," Fred

Gill, an older, ninth-grade student explained, grinning.

But Mike still did not understand. He frowned and started to look back at his assignment. He still felt strange in this new school and at the moment wanted only to be left alone to finish the homework he had been assigned.

"You're famous, Mike," Fred said.

"Famous?"

"Of course."

Mike looked at the still grinning face of Fred Gill. Fred always seemed to have a crowd around him, a gaggle constantly laughing at his wisecracks and pranks. One of Fred's great talents, Mike had noticed, was his ability to find just the right nickname for someone; and the more unkind it was, the greater the chance it would stick. In one of Mike's classes there was a quiet and rather sensitive boy who was known to have real artistic ability—at least from the way the art teacher reacted to his work. This boy had been dubbed "Arty" by Fred Gill, and the name had stuck despite the fact that every time anyone referred to him as Arty the boy would wince visibly, as if he had just been jabbed with a needle.

Was Fred about to sink a needle into him? Mike

67

wondered. And what had he done to gain Fred Gill's unwelcome attention?

"I don't know what you're talking about," said Mike, and again he turned back to his math assignment.

"Oh, sure you do. Don't be modest."

Mike took a deep breath, put down his ballpoint pen, and closed his math book. "Okay," he said. "What is it?"

"You're the brother of Jean Tobin, the first girl in America destined to play for the Houston Astros."

"Imagine how lucky we are to have her in our school," said a boy Mike didn't recognize. The boy was sitting beside Fred Gill.

"We'll all be famous," said another kid.

"May I have your autograph?" asked a third.

"Or better yet," said Fred Gill, "how about you introducing us to your sister?"

"Yeah! We'd like her autograph!"

Mike took a deep breath. He had no intention of sitting still for Fred Gill and his pack. "All right, you guys," he said heavily. "Just back off. Maybe you think you're funny. But I don't."

He had spoken angrily, his voice taking on an unpleasant harshness that caused a few girls further down his table to turn in his direction suddenly.

"Now that's no attitude to take, Mike," protested Fred Gill. He turned to his friends. "Is it, gang?"

They all agreed that it was a very poor attitude indeed for Mike to take, and it was obvious to Mike that they were enjoying themselves immensely.

"Don't tell me," said one of them, "that Mike resents the fact that his sister is a better baseball player than he is!"

"No," said Fred Gill, "you don't resent it at all, do you, Mike."

Mike glanced at the clock on the far wall. There were only a few minutes left, and the cafeteria was rapidly emptying. A few teachers on lunchroom duty were gathered at the far entrance, talking quietly among themselves.

"Why don't you admit it," said another one of the gang. "Your sister is a better ballplayer than you are. I understand she slid in with the winning run last night in the bottom of the sixth. I mean she's a real hero to us all. Don't you agree?"

"She could play rings around you guys, that's for sure," Mike heard himself say. But he hardly recognized his voice. It was tight, and he could feel the blood rushing into his face.

"What shall we call Mike?" Fred Gill asked his

69

friends, as he turned about to consult with them. "How about? . . ."

Just then the bell rang, and Mike got quickly to his feet and launched himself at Fred Gill. Both hands struck the older boy on the shoulders and bore him roughly along the bench and then to the floor as plastic trays clattered noisily down around them. Other classes poured into the cafeteria at the moment the bell rang. The noise of their lining up at the counter, coupled with the continuing shrill call of the second bell, effectively masked the racket Mike and Fred Gill were making as they rolled over and over between the tables.

Mike tried desperately to pull Fred Gill closer to him so he could hammer him, but the older boy kept squealing and pulling away from him. All he could manage was a few glancing blows to the guy's shoulders and head, and then they were out from under the tables in the main aisle. At once the fracas was in plain sight, with teachers streaming toward them from all sides.

Fred Gill was the first to be pulled to his feet by Mr. Reynolds, the assistant principal. Someone else pulled Mike to his feet.

"He's crazy!" Fred Gill said, trembling. "He just jumped on me for no reason at all."

Mike looked at the boy trembling before him and realized at once what an empty threat he really was. "That's a lie," Mike said quietly to Mr. Reynolds. "I had a very good reason for going after him."

"Now that's enough from both of you," the man said. "I think we'd better settle this in my office. Come along."

Fred Gill trotted quickly after Mr. Reynolds, staying as close to him as he could, while Mike followed behind. His mouth was suddenly dry, his heart pounding as the anger that had propelled him at Fred Gill a moment before drained from him.

Following after the assistant principal and Fred Gill down the corridor and past the hushed stares of the students passing to classes, he suddenly remembered his math assignment. He had left the book and the nearly completed work in the cafeteria. If he couldn't find it later, he would have to do all that work over again.

Mike was still thinking of his lost homework assignment when he emerged from the Mr. Reynold's office almost a half hour later and saw Paul DiAngelo coming down the corridor toward him.

The corridor was empty except for them, and Paul

called to Mike. Paul stopped, impatient to get to the cafeteria.

"What do you want?" Mike asked as Paul reached him.

"Hey, I heard all about it. What happened? Did you get kicked out of school?"

"No, I didn't. And what do you mean, you heard all about it?"

"I heard you took on Fred Gill and his gang."

"I wrestled on the cafeteria floor with him for a while, if that's what you mean. It wasn't anything."

"Oh, yeah? You ought to hear the stories that are going around."

"I can bet."

"And Mr. Reynolds didn't kick you out of school?"

"No. He listened to what I told him, and then he called in Fred and listened to his side. When we got through, he warned me that if I ever got into any more trouble with Fred Gill on the school grounds, he would have to punish me severely. But since I was new to the school, he felt that a warning was all that was necessary at this time."

"Hey, he's all right."

"I think he knows all about Fred Gill."

Paul nodded. "That's right. Fred drives all the

teachers crazy. But you sure took care of him today, huh?"

"Look. I've got to go back to the cafeteria and pick up an assignment I left there along with my math book."

"Okay. I'll go with you."

As the two boys hurried down the corridor, Mike wondered why Paul was so friendly all of a sudden. This was a big central school that took care of the whole town, and he had seen Paul plenty of times in the corridors before this. The fellow had just waved and kept right on going. Why, he wondered, was he so interested in him now?

"I heard what it was about," said Paul suddenly as they entered the cafeteria.

"What do you mean?"

"I mean I know why you took after Fred Gill. He was picking on you about Jean. Right?"

Mike saw his math text sitting on the far edge of the now cleared cafeteria table, and beside it was the folded paper he had worked on for so long. Relief flooded over him. He wouldn't have to do the work a second time. As he headed for the book, he told Paul, "Yeah, that's what he was yakking about, all right."

He reached the book and the folded papers, picked

them up, and turned to Paul. "And I don't want to talk about it anymore. I'm late for class now."

Mike's abruptness took Paul by surprise. He took a step back. And there was a frown on his face as he said, "Hey, look, Mike. Don't go confusing me with Fred Gill. I'm a teammate. Remember? I just wanted to let you know that I'm behind you."

"Sure. And you're also the guy who tried to keep Jean off the team."

"And you think I put Fred Gill up to that business about Jean?"

"How do I know you didn't?"

Actually, the thought had not occurred to Mike until the moment Paul suggested the possibility himself. But it did make sense. Those guys with Fred Gill seemed to know an awful lot about that last game.

"Mike, why would I do a thing like that?"

Mike shrugged and turned away from Paul. "I've got to get back to class," he said. "I'm late now. See you around."

Mike hurried from the cafeteria, leaving Paul standing there.

"Mike! Mike! Wait for me!"

Mike turned and saw his sister trying to catch up with him.

74

"What did you hurry off like that for? Why didn't you wait?" she asked when, puffing slightly, she finally caught up with Mike.

"Well, golly . . . I don't want to be always hanging around, waiting for you."

"Okay. I can see that. But you've got to tell me what happened today in school. You should hear the crazy stories I'm hearing."

"Fred Gill was shooting his mouth off. He got me mad, so I . . . took a swing at him, that's all."

"It was about me, wasn't it." Jean did not ask this. She stated it as a fact.

"It was about you, all right. According to him, I'm famous because I'm *your* brother."

Jean's face became somewhat grim. "Go on," she said.

"You're the first girl to play for the Houston Astros, and I shouldn't be jealous because you are a better ballplayer than I am."

"I'd like to slap his face."

Mike grinned suddenly. "And I'd like to see you do it. Trouble is, if you did, he'd just break down and cry."

"I never did like that creep and that pack that travels with him. But what about Mr. Reynolds? Are you in any kind of trouble with him?"

Mike explained then what had happened in the

assistant principal's office, and he and Jean started up again. Jean was quiet for a while, but she had a puzzled frown on her face. Suddenly she stopped.

Mike stopped and looked at her. "What's wrong?"

"You don't believe that, do you?"

"Believe what."

"That I'm a better ballplayer than you are."

"Well, you played the whole game, while I sat it out on the bench."

"That was just one game."

"You got two singles, one in the second inning and one in the sixth; and you slid home with the winning run. I missed a fly ball I should have caught and struck out and grounded out."

"Mike, that was just the first game. We've got a whole *season* yet."

"It looks more like you've got the season."

"Are you going to believe that creep, Fred Gill? Honestly!"

He looked at her sharply. "Okay then. I'm a better ballplayer than you are. Is that what *you* think?"

"Well now, I didn't say that—not exactly."

Mike laughed. And then Jean laughed along with him. As they started up again, Mike had an idea.

"There's one way to settle this. As soon as we get changed, let's go over to the park for a game of scrub. The first one to knock it into the trees wins."

"From where."

"The plate in front of the backstop."

"Okay."

Mike felt better at once. He knew he could hit the ball farther than Jean. He always had been able to do so in the past and saw no reason why he couldn't do so now. And Jean was right, after all. That game the other night was just the first game of a long, long season. And once Mike got his batting eye and settled down in the outfield, he would be in every game.

"Hey," said Jean. "Here comes a crowd of kids from the next street over. I'll stop to tie my shoelaces and you go ahead. You don't want them to think you're always with your crazy old sister."

As Jean put her books down on the sidewalk and bent over to fumble with her shoelaces, Mike walked on ahead past the crowd of kids, suddenly grateful that he had a sister who really understood about this sort of thing. It was with a pang of guilt that he recalled his earlier resentment of Jean's success on the Dolphins.

But he sure hoped he played in the next game.

7

MIKE REACHED UP and caught the ball, transferred it to his throwing hand, and threw it back toward the bat Jean had dropped to the ground. It bounced twice, then straightened out and began to roll right for the bat until—at the last possible moment—it struck a hummock of grass and hopped over the handle.

"Too bad!" Jean called as she pounced on the ball and then picked up the bat.

Mike punched his glove and waited for her to hit the ball back to him. They had decided they wouldn't count fly balls that were caught. The only way to get up was to hit the bat. And that would give them both plenty of opportunity to see who could hit the ball the farthest. The only trouble was

78

that so far, Jean was the only one who had batted. Mike had lost the toss, and Jean had stayed at bat for almost a half hour.

But she had not yet been able to drive him into the trees, and that last one he had caught was well in front of them. He crouched, waiting for her next fly.

Jean tossed the ball into the air and brought her bat around. This was a good one, he realized, as he raced back toward the trees. But then Mike saw that it was going to fall short. He pulled up, came in, caught the ball easily, and then waited for Jean to put the bat down.

He could see it clearly from where he stood. His eye on it all the way, he wound up and threw the ball in, being careful this time to concentrate on accuracy rather than speed. The ball began to roll sooner than before, and it looked as if the grass would slow it to a halt before it reached the bat. But the ball kept going . . . and going. And then it hopped into the air as it struck the fat part of the bat, the *thunk* it made carrying all the way out to Mike.

"Now you watch!" cried Mike as he raced in to bat.

"Okay," replied Jean, trotting past him. "We'll see."

Mike tried his best, but his first fly ball to Jean was too high for any real distance. Jean ran in and camped under it. There was a smile on her face when she caught it and waited for Mike to drop the bat.

"You'll miss it," Mike assured her.

She threw carefully, and for a moment it looked as if the ball was going directly for the bat. But it hit a rock or something and veered off course. When it had passed the bat, Mike picked it up.

"You'd better get back now!" he warned Jean. "Here it goes!"

On his second try he really got the good wood on the ball, but again—though the ball was hit very high —it simply did not have the distance. Again Jean caught the ball easily and threw it in. This time she was wide of the mark.

As Mike bent to pick up the ball, he saw a familiar figure moving across the grass toward him. Paul DiAngelo. He nodded curtly to the boy, then tossed the ball and hit it as hard as he could.

This time it was not only hit high, it was also hit far; and he smiled as he saw Jean, looking back over a shoulder as she ran, retreating further and further. Just before the trees, however, she reached up and caught the fly in full stride.

Watching Jean with his hands on his hips, Paul DiAngelo shook his head in admiration. "Some catch," he said.

"That's right," said Mike. "And she probably won't play major league ball someday."

"Okay. Okay," said Paul, putting up his hand. "Jean's on the team now. We voted on it, and that's that. Can't you let what I said rest?"

That was a fair question, all right. Besides, Mike had a good opinion of Paul as a ballplayer. He shrugged and smiled. "It's a deal."

"And I didn't have anything to do with Fred Gill bugging you in school today."

"I was just upset."

The ball came in from Jean. It was a good throw, but at least a foot to one side of the bat. As Mike picked up the ball, he explained to Paul what they were playing.

"It's scrub. If you hit the bat with the ball after you catch it, you get to bat. Right now we got a bet on about who can hit it into the trees on the fly first."

"You almost did that last time."

"I will this time. Watch."

But again Mike got under the ball a little too much, and Jean had no trouble running in a few steps and catching it. As Mike dropped the bat for his sister, he felt a buildup of frustration. He certainly wasn't going to prove he was a better ballplayer than his sister at this rate. Why couldn't he reach those trees?

"Mind if I make a suggestion, Mike?" asked Paul. "Go ahead."

"Hitting the ball this way is not very good practice for hitting a pitched ball."

Mike watched the ball rolling over the ground toward the bat lying at his feet. "Is that so?"

"It's a lot of fun, I admit. But you—and Jean too —need practice hitting a pitched ball."

The ball hopped over the bat. Mike picked it up and reached down for the bat. Resting it lightly on his shoulder, he looked at Paul. "Jean's been hitting the ball all right, I noticed. She got two hits in the game, didn't she?"

"She was lucky. She swung late on both of them and was lucky to get the ball into the air and over the infield."

"A lot of other guys probably wished they could be so lucky."

"Look. You can go ahead and play like this if you want. I'm only trying to help, for crying out loud."

Mike shrugged. "Okay, then. Go ahead. Help."

Paul shook his head. "Boy, you sure don't make it easy for a guy to be friendly, do you."

Mike took a big breath. "Maybe not, but Jean and I have been playing ball with each other as long as I can remember. And where we came from, we were the best around."

"Well, look. All I'm trying to do is help you to hit good pitching. You probably didn't see much of it where you came from."

Mike didn't like that. There were a lot of kids in Sterling Valley who could really pitch. But he kept himself from saying anything about that. "Go ahead, then," Mike repeated. "Show me how."

"Call in Jean."

Mike waved to Jean, and she started in.

"I'll pitch to you and Jean in front of the backstop while one of you shags. I can show you what I mean that way."

"Batting practice."

"That's right."

As Jean pulled up beside them, Mike said, "Paul thinks we don't know how to hit a well-pitched ball, but he's going to show us how. He thinks hitting the ball this way is bad for us."

"It really is, Jean," said Paul. "What I mean is that you should practice hitting pitched balls, too."

Jean looked at Mike. "Makes sense, I guess. Do you want to bat first, Mike?"

Mike shrugged. "I don't care."

"Sure you do," she said, laughing. "Okay. I'll shag." She turned and trotted back out into the outfield.

Paul stuck his hand into the well-worn outfielder's

glove he carried and tugged his baseball cap more firmly down over his forehead. Mike tossed him the baseball and started for the backstop.

When he got himself dug in before it, Paul threw him a medium fast pitch. Mike swung, lunging clumsily forward, and missed. As he picked up the ball and fired it back at Paul, he felt a tingle of embarrassment. He certainly had not looked very good on that pitch—and it had been right over.

"See what you're doing?" said Paul.

"No, I don't," replied Mike, just a bit irritated at Paul's question.

"You swung up at it, the way you swing at those balls you toss into the air. You've got to hold your shoulders level and swing level. And maybe you shouldn't stride all that much."

"How's that again?"

Paul grinned. "Okay. Let's take one thing at a time. Hold your bat back and try to keep your shoulders level when you swing—a level swing is what you want. Just try to hit line drives."

But on the next pitch Mike dropped one shoulder and tried to get under the ball to lift it into the trees. He got just a piece of the ball and sent a soft bloop back to Paul, who caught it easily.

"See what I mean?" said Paul, grinning.

"Well, how do you know all this?"

"My uncle. He played in the majors for a while. He's worked out with me."

Mike nodded grimly. "Okay. So I keep my shoulders level."

"And spread your legs a little, so you don't stride so far."

"Like this?"

"That's right. Do you feel comfortable?"

Mike thought about it. "Yes," he admitted. "I feel comfortable. But how am I going to remember all this when I'm swinging at the ball?"

Paul nodded in appreciation of Mike's dilemma. "You won't be able to—at first."

"Hey, let's go!" cried Jean from the outfield. "I'm falling asleep out here while you two jabber."

Paul threw the ball at Mike. It was a good pitch, and Mike wanted to really loft it by getting under it, but he controlled the impulse and concentrated on hitting the ball on a level. To his surprise he connected solidly and sent the ball deep and on a line toward Jean.

Jean took a few steps in, then reversed herself, backpedaled frantically, and stuck up her glove. She caught the ball, but it was the best hit ball Mike had managed in a long long time.

He looked at Paul with new respect. He knew the fellow was a ball hawk; he had noticed that the first day he had seen him in the field. But now it was obvious that Paul really knew what he was talking about when it came to hitting the ball.

As Paul turned to catch Jean's throw, he yelled out to her, "How was that? You awake now?"

"Okay," she called to him. "Let's see Mike do it again."

Paul turned back to Mike. "Another thing, Mike. Try to hit the ball while it is in front of you and see if you can see the ball hitting the bat."

Mike shrugged. It sounded a little difficult, but he would sure give it a try.

Paul's pitch was a little high and inside the next time, and Mike was not able to hit it. But on Paul's next serve, Mike swung as before, caught the ball well out in front of the plate, and actually did manage to see the ball the moment it met the bat. As he followed through he felt the solid tingle of the bat and knew he had hit the ball with even more power than before.

Again it rose only slowly as it carried far toward the trees. Jean was running full out this time as she tried to get under the ball, but at the last moment she pulled up rather than keep running into the trees. The ball landed well beyond her and bounced out of sight.

He had finally reached the trees, but not by trying to lift the ball.

"Hey," he told Paul. "Let's try that again."

"Sure," said Paul. "But don't expect to hit them all like that from now on. It's going to take practice to get your swing back to normal."

But when, an hour later, Mike and Jean walked back to their house, Mike was jubilant. Jean too was excited, though not to the extent that Mike was. Both of them had noticed a significant improvement in their batting as a result of the advice given them by Paul DiAngelo. But Mike's improvement was by far the most spectacular. He had placed three balls well into the trees on the fly.

"If I could hit like that tonight," Mike said, "I wouldn't have any trouble at all making the team."

"You won't have any trouble, anyway, Mike. The only reason you didn't play the whole game the other night was because the coach wanted to look at everyone he had on the roster."

"Then why didn't he put Skip Wiesmann in?"

She shrugged. "Well . . . I don't know, but I'm sure you won't have any trouble at all making the team."

"That's what I thought too, but now I'm not so

87

sure. *You* won't have any trouble, but it sure looks like I might—unless I can keep hitting like I was just now." Suddenly he grinned at her. "Hey, are you forgetting why we went over to the field?"

"Nope."

"And I was the first one to knock the ball into the trees."

"Yes, you were."

"So that proves it."

"I suppose so."

"What do you mean, you *suppose* so. That was our bet, wasn't it?"

"Okay. You win."

Mike took a deep breath. "Boy, I can't wait for the next game now. And I sure hope Fred Gill is in the stands."

Jean didn't respond as she continued to walk beside him in silence.

After a while, Mike noticed her silence and said, "You shouldn't feel bad, Sis. I'll bet you can hit the ball better than any girl in the country."

"Thanks, Mike. It's real nice to have you in my corner."

"That's okay."

And though they walked the rest of the way home in silence, Mike didn't really notice. He was thinking

88

of the way he had been hitting the ball while Paul DiAngelo had pitched to him and was already dreaming ahead to the next ball game.

Mr. Franklin sure had better let him play now.

8

MIKE WAS WATCHING television in the middle of the living room floor with his head resting on a pillow when he heard the kitchen door open, followed by the heavy thump of his father's suitcase. As his father approached the living room archway, Mike propped himself up on his elbows.

"Hey, isn't this Thursday?" the man asked in surprise.

"Sure," Mike replied. "It's Thursday. Welcome back, Dad. How was the trip?"

"You know how I feel about long business trips, Mike. But aren't you supposed to be playing tonight? I hurried home and grabbed a bite on the way, so I wouldn't miss the game tonight."

Mike looked back at the TV set, his head resting again on the pillow. "You won't miss the game."

90

"But aren't you playing?"

"No. But Jean is."

At that moment Mike's mother hurried downstairs and greeted Mike's father. Mike kept his eyes on the TV set and hoped they would both go away.

"Mike?"

Mike turned back to look at his father. "Yes, Dad?"

"I'd like to go watch the game. Are you coming with us?"

"I don't feel like it, Dad. For the last two weeks all I've been doing is sitting on the bench watching Jean play. Sometimes I get to play a few innings and sometimes I don't. I get more playing done after school when I work out with a few of the players, but mostly all I do at games is sit."

"I see. Well, that's up to you then. Are you quitting the team?"

"I'm thinking about it."

Mike's father stood in the living room doorway looking down unhappily at his son. Mike could tell he didn't really know what to say. His father was disappointed, of that Mike was certain. But then, so was Mike. He was a much better hitter than when the season began, and a better outfielder, too. Paul DiAngelo made one fine coach. He didn't just stand around and tell you to hit the ball better or catch

91

the ball better, he actually *showed* a guy how to do it.

But the fact of the matter was that the Dolphins didn't need him. They had Jean at third, and they were winning. And that was all that mattered.

"Well . . . your mother and I are going down to the ball park to watch Jean play. You are welcome to come along if you want."

"No, thanks, Dad. You go along. I've got some homework I've got to finish anyway."

Mike turned off the TV as soon as they left the house and went upstairs. From his window he watched the car back out of the driveway and turn down the street in the direction of the Little League park. He looked out the window at the town that was so different and so far away from Sterling Valley. He remembered how miserable he had felt when he had first moved to Addison, and then how much better he had felt when he thought he was going to play on the Dolphins.

But now he was right back where he started, looking out the window and thinking of Sterling Valley.

Abruptly, Mike turned from the window. What

was the matter with him anyway, moping around like this? He had some homework to do, so he'd better get to it and stop feeling sorry for himself.

He sat down at his desk, turned on his lamp, and got busy.

"Hey, Mike! Hold up!"

Mike turned to see Paul DiAngelo hurrying down the street toward him. He stopped and waited for Paul to catch up.

"You weren't at the game last night."

"That's right," Mike said.

"How come?"

"I had some homework to do and didn't feel like riding the bench anymore."

"You're not quitting, are you?"

"Might as well."

"I wish you wouldn't."

"Why not? I'm not doing the team any good just sitting on the bench."

"Well, I wish you wouldn't. I think it would make Jean feel awful if she felt . . . well, you know."

Mike was surprised at Paul's concern about Jean. At the same time he realized that the fellow was right. If he did quit the team, it would be like leaving Jean

93

high and dry. But to sit there and watch *her* play, while he . . .

"How come you're so concerned about Jean?" Mike asked. "Don't tell me you think girls should play baseball after all."

"She's just a member of the team," Paul protested. "That's all. Say, how come you're going home this way?"

Mike shrugged. He didn't want to tell Paul the real reason, which was that it was a different route from the one his sister took, and that he just felt more comfortable walking home alone lately. For the same reason, he now made sure that his sister left before him in the morning. He was sure Jean understood it was nothing personal.

"How about practice? Steve Deforrest told me he'd meet me at the field around three."

"Sure."

"Okay. Get Jean and that'll give us four, enough for a good batting practice session."

Mike stopped. "Look. Do I have to go home and get Jean? She played last night, didn't she? Someone else will probably show up anyway."

Paul shrugged. "Suit yourself. But won't she see you getting your glove and stuff? She'll want to come along too, won't she?"

"I don't have to go home. I can play in these clothes easily enough. And I can borrow a glove from somebody."

"Okay. But I don't live far from here. Come home with me so I can get my stuff. It won't take long."

As Mike cut down the side street with Paul, he felt just a little conspiratorial. But it was not an unpleasant feeling. It felt good, in fact, to be able to fix it so that—at least for this one time—*he* would be playing and not Jean.

And he didn't care how disloyal that sounded.

When he arrived home finally—weary and sweat streaked from an exhausting but thoroughly enjoyable session of batting and shagging—he was almost too late for supper. His place at the table was still set, but his mother was in the act of clearing off the rest of the supper dishes.

"Sorry I'm late, Mom," he said, as he slipped into his chair.

His father, heading into the living room with the evening paper in his hand, glanced at him and said, "Next time, if you're going to be as late as this, call home. I've told you before about that."

"Okay, Dad."

Jean was just finishing up her dessert of butter-scotch pudding. She glanced across the table at Mike. "Hi, Mike."

"Hi, Jean."

Mike looked quickly, guiltily away from her face and looked up at his mother as she brought him his plate. As he caught a whiff of the meat, potatoes, and gravy, he realized in that instant how ravenously hungry he was and set to work with a will.

He was alone at a cleared and immaculate table when at last he finished his second helping of butter-scotch pudding.

"Stay there," said his mother, as she picked up his dish and spoon. "I want to talk to you."

There was something in her tone that warned Mike to get ready for some serious conversation. And the look on her face when she sat down across from him a moment later only confirmed that expectation.

"What's happening to you and Jean?" his mother asked abruptly. "You two are like strangers. You never talk. In the morning she sneaks out ahead of you, and only when she's well on her way do you dare to set out. The two of you used to be such . . . good friends, I thought. Now you hardly talk. It's this baseball business, isn't it."

96

"Mom, you're just imagining things. I can't always be hanging around my sister, for crying out loud. I mean . . . well, golly. I have my own friends, don't forget." But all the time he was speaking, he didn't look into his mother's eyes.

"It's this baseball. I knew it."

Mike started to deny it, but didn't have the heart to lie to his mother. He looked away from her and said nothing.

His mother sighed and got up. "I cannot *make* you two act sensibly," she said. "But I wish you would realize that baseball is just a game."

"Yes, Mom."

"You have homework?"

Mike nodded.

"Final exams coming up?"

"This Friday and the first of next week."

"So you'd better study then, and forget this baseball, I'm thinking."

Mike got up, left the kitchen, and hurried up the stairs to his room. As he passed his sister's room, he saw that her door was opened slightly. He hesitated. It took him just a second to make up his mind. He knocked on the door.

"Come in, Mike."

Mike pushed the door open and walked into his

sister's room. She was at her desk, turned in her chair so as to face him.

"Just came in to ask you about the game last night. Understand you did pretty well."

"I got a hit in the fifth."

"And Paul said you made a nice backhand stab of a hard bouncer for a force at second base."

"Paul DiAngelo?"

"That's right. He's getting to be a fan of yours."

"That's a switch."

"Yeah."

Mike took a deep breath. There seemed to be nothing more to say. "Well . . . nice going anyway."

As he started to leave, Jean said, "Mike, are you quitting the team?"

"Quitting the team?"

"That's right."

Mike shrugged. "Oh . . . I don't know. Maybe. I'm not sure. You guys are doing all right without me, only a game out of first place."

"That's nothing. It's going to be a long season."

"I suppose."

"I wish you wouldn't quit, Mike."

"Well . . . maybe I won't."

"Did Mom talk to you?"

Mike nodded.

"Me too. She reminded me that baseball was just a game—nothing to lose a friend over."

"Now listen," Mike said hastily. "No one's lost any friends over baseball."

"And you won't quit?"

"No," Mike said, taking the plunge. "I'm not quitting." He felt better the moment the words left his mouth.

"That's fine," Jean said.

She turned back to her desk and the pile of books waiting for her. She had finals to get ready for too, it appeared.

The next practice was Saturday morning, two days later. As Mike turned off the sidewalk and started across the grass, he noticed a white van pulled up in back of the backstop. As he got closer he read the large red letters on the side of the van:

W G B H
CHANNEL ELEVEN
YOUR LOCAL ABC AFFILIATE

From the rear of the van streamed a dark river of coiling lines and cables leading to a series of tripods and cameras that had been set up around home plate and third base. Technicians in white coveralls and baseball caps were working with the cameras and checking the cables, while others were continually hopping in and out of the rear of the van.

A man Mike did not recognize was talking to Coach Franklin, and as Mike neared him, he could see that the coach was not at all pleased with what was going on.

Before Mike got much closer, Steve Deforrest ran up to him. "Hey! We're all going to be on television!"

"How come?"

"You're famous—or rather, Jean is. There was something in the morning paper about our Little League not getting an official charter from Williamsport because of a girl on one of our teams."

"Not getting a charter?"

"That's right. So the station wants to do a spot on us for tonight's news show."

Mike moved quickly past Steve, right up to Mr. Franklin, who was still talking to the fellow from the station. "Mr. Franklin," he said. "Is this true? Aren't we going to get a charter?"

"That's not true at all. I haven't heard a thing from Williamsport. I sent it in rather late because some of our teams didn't get organized in time, so that's the only reason for the delay as far as I can see."

"Sure," said the fellow from the station, "but it's a great story, anyway. A girl on third!"

"Well, if you don't mind," Mr. Franklin said. "Since there's no truth in that news item, we'd like you to get your cameras and your sound truck out of here so we can have our practice."

"It won't take long. Just a few shots. We'd like one of the girl at bat and fielding a ground ball at third. And I understand she's got a brother she bounced off the team."

Mike felt his face go scarlet.

"This is her brother right here," Mr. Franklin said, "and his sister did *not* bounce him off the team. He hasn't played regularly, but there are other reasons for that."

"Are you Mike Tobin?" the TV director asked.

Mike nodded.

"Well, how about coming over here for a quick interview. It won't take a second, and you'll be able to see yourself on TV on the news show this evening."

Mike looked at Coach Franklin. "Do I have to?"

"Not if you don't want to," the coach replied firmly.

Mike looked back at the director. "I don't want to be on your news show."

The fellow tried to keep his smile intact, but it was

plain that he had not expected this kind of a reaction. He looked back at Mr. Franklin.

"Come on, Coach," he said. "Tell him. We won't hurt him. And he'll be a local celebrity."

"That may not be what the boy wants," Mr. Franklin said, and Mike could see that the coach's face was getting brick red in annoyance.

The director shrugged. "Okay." He looked around. "Where's the girl? We'll take a short interview with her and leave."

Mike looked around. He had left the house before Jean, and she still hadn't shown up. He had an idea. "I'll go see what's holding her up," he said.

He turned and hurried off the field and started down the street in the direction of his house. He had gone almost a full block when he saw her coming, her pigtails tucked under her cap, her baseball bat resting on her shoulder, her glove dangling from the handle. He waved to her to stop. Then he ran toward her.

"What's up?" Jean asked, as soon as Mike reached her.

"There's a whole mess of guys with cameras and a sound truck and everything from Channel Eleven waiting for you at the ball park. They want to interview us because you're a girl playing on a Little League team."

102

"Wait a minute! Wait a minute," Jean exclaimed, putting her hand up. "Slow down. I didn't get all that."

Slower this time, Mike explained what was waiting for them at the ball park and also alerted her to the rumor that because of her presence on the team, the town was in danger of not getting its official Little League charter from Williamsport.

When he had finished, Jean brought the bat down from her shoulder and looked at him for a long moment. Then she shook her head. "I think I'll miss practice today," she said.

"Well, that's why I ran back here to meet you. I wanted to warn you."

"And I better not go home. They'll find me there if I do."

"You could hide in the woods in back of the outfield."

"This is ridiculous."

"I know."

"I'll go over to Paula Freeman's house. She's in my earth science class, and she says she wants help in it. I'll stay there all morning or until the coast is clear."

"Okay."

"Tell Coach Franklin I'm sorry for missing practice."

"Don't worry. He understands. I don't think he likes the idea of those guys coming down like that and disrupting practice."

"Here," she said. "Take my bat and glove. I won't be needing it."

She handed the bat and glove to Mike, then turned and walked off. Mike could tell from the set of her shoulders how angry she was. He watched her go for a few seconds, then turned and started back to the park.

He would just tell Mr. Franklin she wasn't coming, and the coach would understand. He wouldn't tell the TV director anything.

9

"WELL, I MUST ADMIT I'm surprised," said Mike's mother as she began to clear away the supper dishes. "Imagine refusing to be on television."

"Most kids," said Mike's father, his eyes twinkling in appreciation of what Mike and Jean had just finished telling, "would jump at the opportunity to become famous TV celebrities."

"Maybe," said Mike.

"Well," said Jean firmly, "I sure wasn't anxious for any local celebrity status. You know the kind of questions some of those TV reporters ask."

"What do you mean, dear?" asked Jean's mother.

"Oh, you know. They'd probably ask me how it felt to be on a team loaded with boys . . . or if I was striking a blow for the female race . . . and did I really

105

think I was as good as a boy . . . that kind of stuff."

"Oh, I don't think so," her mother said.

Mike spoke up then. "Mom, the fellow that was talking to the coach told him he understood that Jean had a brother she bounced off the team. Then he wanted to interview me."

"Yes," said Mike's father thoughtfully, his brows suddenly knitting, "I can just imagine that fellow's questions."

"Oh, Mike . . ." said Jean. "You didn't tell me he said that. What else did he say?"

"That's all he got a chance to say. I was standing right there, and Mr. Franklin denied it. He said there were other reasons I hadn't played regularly."

"Oh?" said his father. "And what were the reasons he gave?"

"He didn't give any. That was when the TV director tried to get me in front of one of the cameras."

"Well," said Mike's father. "You know, you can't hide from their news cameras indefinitely. There's nothing to stop them from putting up cameras during tonight's game, taking all the footage, and making all the interviews they want."

"Oh, golly," said Mike. "I suppose that's true."

"I was wondering about that," admitted Jean.

"Come on," said Mike's father. "Let's all drive down to the park together for tonight's game—the four Tobins, united and indestructible."

Jean's mother brightened as she untied her apron and slipped it over her head. "That's a fine idea," she said. "Jean, give me a hand putting the rest of these dishes away."

But when they pulled up at the Little League park, there was no large white van.

"Not enough light for their TV cameras," Mr. Tobin said. "I'll bet that's it."

"Whatever the reason, it makes me feel a whole lot better not to see them."

But it turned out there were other distractions. The Dolphins were playing the Yankees, and the crowd of spectators in the stands behind the Yankee bench seemed unusually large—and noisy. The reason for this was soon obvious.

"Oh, boy," said Mike to Jean, as they approached the Dolphin bench. "Look at that sign."

WE WANT A CHARTER
NOT A TOMBOY!!!

107

"I don't think they used enough exclamation points," Jean remarked as she leaned her bat against the bench.

By now Jean was in plain sight, and her appearance seemed to galvanize the spectators. The sign Jean and Mike had just read was brought down by the two people carrying it and was paraded up and down in front of the stands while the spectators cheered.

Then another sign wriggled to life, and the two girls carrying it hurried down to fall in step behind the first one. This one read:

GIRLS SHOULD JUMP
ROPE.

And as soon as this sign had been paraded around for a few minutes, crossing twice in front of the Yankee bench, another sign was brought down for display:

SOFTBALL IS FOR GIRLS.
BASEBALL IS FOR BOYS!

Jean was having batting practice when this sign appeared. She swung at a pitch and fouled it into the ground. Then she turned to the Yankee bench and shrugged—as if to say maybe that last sign was right.

But on the next pitch, she cut viciously and sent a screaming liner into right field. Mike, playing catch with Steve Deforrest in foul territory down the right field line, watched it skip along past the lunging glove of . lly Cashman and grinned at Steve.

"Boy, if Jean's mad, she'll play all the better."

"I hope so," replied Steve as he hauled down Mike's throw. "The Yankee's are in first place."

And the Yankees were tough. They were impressive both in the field and at bat. Their infielders and outfielders took turns robbing Dolphin batters of hits, while they scored three runs in the first two innings, and then knocked Paul Swenson out of the game in the third by scoring three more.

But in the bottom of the third, the Dolphins roared back to score four runs of their own and chase the Yankee pitcher.

Jean made the last out by flying to center, and as the players grabbed their gloves and headed for their positions, Coach Franklin pulled Mike to one side.

"Mike, you've been missing practices lately and you have also missed games."

"I know it, Mr. Franklin."

"Are you back now to stay?"

"Yes, I am, Coach."

"Good. It looks to me like your batting has improved some, at least from the way you've been hitting the ball in pregame practice, and Paul DiAngelo tells me he's been working out with you a lot."

Mike nodded.

"You're only eleven, Mark. Billy Cashman and Lee Wagner are both twelve. This is their last year as Little Leaguers—their first and their last. So I've given them the edge. But if you can hit as well as they can and field as well as they do, then I'll just have to play you. Is that clear?"

"Yes, Coach."

"Okay, then. Go in for Billy Cashman in right."

That had been a long conversation, and as Mike raced out into right field, Coach Franklin had to call time to allow Mike to get into position. As Billy saw Mike coming, he put his head down and raced in.

As he passed Mike, he called, "Good luck, Mike!"

"Okay now, let's hold 'em!" called Paul DiAngelo from center field.

Mike punched his glove and nodded.

Al Dekin was pitching now, and Paul Swenson was playing second in his place. Al was pretty good. He had started pitching a few games back, Mike remembered, and had done all right.

110

He started out fine this inning, too. He got two quick fast strikes on the first batter, wasted a few low and outside, then came in with another fast ball. The batter swung and missed and went back to the bench muttering to himself.

The second batter lofted a short one to center, but Paul was "on his horse" the moment the ball left the bat. Loping in easily, he put it away for the second out of the inning.

The third batter managed a couple of long fouls, then laced an inside pitch that nearly took Jean's glove off as she flagged it down. But she hung on to the ball and tossed it lightly toward the mound as she trotted in to the Dolphin bench.

"Heck," said Paul DiAngelo, as he trotted in toward the bench beside Mike, "if that doesn't shut up those Yankee wolves, nothing will."

"I don't expect anything will, Paul," Mike said.

The center fielder just shook his head.

From the first inning on, both the spectators in the stands behind the Yankee bench and the Yankee players themselves had really been unloading on Jean. Every move she made was followed with a shout or a cry. If a ball was hit to her, there would be an immediate outcry. Even after a good play, cries of "You were lucky!" would soar out over the little park.

And in the second inning when she had struck out there were cheers and whistles from the stands. In fact, so intense was the feeling that came from the stands at that time that the Yankee players themselves had motioned to their frenzied supporters to cool it.

But throughout the uproar Jean gave no indication that she was experiencing anything at all unusual. She went about her duties as third baseman for the Dolphins as calmly as if she were still back in Sterling Valley playing ball with her friends. But as Mike watched her he knew she must be feeling something deep inside her. She just had too much guts to let on. He looked back occasionally at his parents in the stands. Their faces were grim, but also, Mike thought, proud.

"This team thinks they're going to win it all, Mike," explained Paul DiAngelo at one point when the bench jockeying got pretty rough, "so they're worried that with Jean on our roster, they won't be able to get a charter and go to the state finals in August."

Mike nodded grimly and at the same time hoped fervently that the Yankees did not win it all. And they wouldn't if he had anything to say about it.

And now he was in the lineup against them.

Steve Deforrest flied out, and Swenson hit the ball

sharply but right at the first baseman, who fielded the ball in his big glove and stepped on first.

Mike left the on-deck circle, walked around behind the catcher, and dug himself into the batter's box. By now he was using a wider stance than before and was careful to anchor his rear foot. As he was getting himself set, the catcher tried to rattle him by mentioning how much better a ballplayer his sister was, but Mike paid the catcher no heed. This too he had learned from Paul. It was the catcher's job, as Paul explained, to shake up the batter. It was the batter's job to ignore him and wait for his pitch.

And the first pitch to Mike was low and outside. Mike watched it go by. Ball one. The next pitch was right down the pipe, however, and Mike swung. He got a piece of it and slammed it foul.

One ball, one strike.

"Hey, Mike, let's see if you can hit as good as your sister!"

Mike glanced at the Yankee bench, then back at the pitcher. The fellow was already well into his windup and pitched just as Mike looked back. The pitch looked a little outside, but Mike wasn't sure. He swung at it halfheartedly and caught the ball on the end of his bat, dribbling a grounder out in front of the plate.

He put his head down and ran as fast as he could,

but the ball whistled over his head and into the first baseman's glove before he was halfway down the line.

As he trotted over to the bench to get his glove, he kept his eyes down. He had let them rattle him. Some yokel had yelled at him, and he had taken his eye off the pitcher. They couldn't rattle his sister, but they sure had no trouble rattling him.

He slipped his glove over his left hand and ran quickly out to his position. As he got himself set, he glanced over at Paul DiAngelo. The center fielder kept his gaze straight ahead as Al Dekin finished his warm-up. Mike looked in and punched his glove.

With the score six to four in favor of the Yankees, they couldn't let the Yankees get any more runs. That was why Mike groaned when the first batter up singled sharply to center.

Then Al walked the next batter. Two men on, no one out.

"Okay! Get two, you guys!" Mike yelled.

"That's the way to holler," said Paul DiAngelo, calling over to him. "Better get back a little for this next batter. He hit a pretty long one in the first."

Mike moved back promptly, then set himself as Al Dekin pitched. The batter swung and connected, sending the ball on a line into right center. Mike was off the moment the ball began its flight; and when he saw Paul heading over just as fast to flag

114

the ball down, he yelled, "It's my ball! I got it! I got it!"

Paul pulled up quickly and then raced back behind Mike as Mike reached up for the ball, caught it in full stride, and then fired to third. The runner on second had tagged up and now bluffed a run to third. But Mike's throw was perfect. Jean caught the ball on the first hop and fired it over to second. The runner was lucky to get back in time.

"Nice peg, Mike!" Paul called over to him.

Mike acknowledged the compliment with a wave. He felt much better all of a sudden.

The next batter sent a high pop over the infield, which Pete Ceballo caught easily.

Two outs. Mike punched his glove and then put it up to his mouth.

"That's the way to pitch in there, Al!"

"Two down, fellows!" Paul DiAngelo called in. "Play at any three bases!"

Al pitched. The ball was low, but over the plate. The batter swung and sent a dribbler to second. Swenson fielded the ball cleanly and went to first to end the scoring threat.

"Now that was nice pitching," Paul commented to Mike as they trotted in. "The first two men got on but didn't score. Very nice indeed. Looks like we found ourselves a pitcher."

"Now if we can just get some runs."

Paul nodded.

As Lee Wagner selected a bat and headed for the plate, Coach Franklin stopped beside Mike in front of the bench. "That was a nice catch, Mike," he said, "and a fine peg in to third."

Before Mike could get a chance to thank the coach, the sharp crack of a bat brought their attention back to the ball game. Mike looked up in time to see a line drive falling into center as Lee Wagner raced down the line to first with a lead-off single.

Paul DiAngelo left the on-deck circle and approached the batter's box. Jean's voice could be heard along with Al Dekin's and Bob Corbett's, urging Paul to hit a long one. Mike joined the chorus.

Paul tugged on the visor of his cap and then took one slow practice cut. The Yankee pitcher fired the ball. It was inside and low, and Paul glanced at it almost contemptuously as it went by.

Mike smiled. Paul was a real cool one, all right. He had already doubled sharply off the other Yankee pitcher, though with the sacks empty and no one behind him capable of pushing him around. Now, at last, there was a duck on the pond, and he represented the tying run.

116

The next pitch was a little high, and he did not offer at it. The umpire called it a strike. Paul didn't react. He just took another practice swing and waited for the next pitch.

It looked like a curve to Mike and seemed to break right over the plate. Paul swung. He caught the ball on the fat part of the bat and followed through completely. The crack was a solid one, and Mike jumped up with everyone else to watch as the ball kept rising. The right fielder started to race back desperately, and then he pulled up and watched as the ball sailed well into the trees that bordered the park.

According to the ground rules settled on before the game, it was a home run!

That made it six to six, and it looked as if a fine rally were in progress. But the next three batters went out in order, and the sixth inning began with a ball game all tied up.

Al Dekin pitched carefully to the first Yankee batter to face him, and as a result he walked him. The Yankee bench really opened up on Al after that, but he paid little heed as he struck out the next batter and made the next two ground out routinely to the infield.

As Jean selected a bat and started for the plate, the noise that came from the stands back of the Yankee

117

bench rose to a crescendo. Mike compressed his lips and tried to ignore it. Paul DiAngelo was sitting alongside of him on the bench.

"She'll get a hit. You watch," he said.

"Anything to shut those wolves up," Mike replied, glancing over at the spectators. Even as he looked, he saw those two girls bringing down their sign about the desirability of girls sticking to jumping rope. But Jean apparently gave no indication she saw or heard anything unusual as she settled herself in at the plate and waited for the first pitch.

It was inside, and she ducked back almost casually.

"She's a cool one," said Paul.

The next pitch was right down the alley, and Jean ripped into it. The ball left her bat on a line and traveled over the lunging second baseman's glove. So hard was the ball hit that it seemed to increase in speed as soon as it struck the outfield. Both Yankee fielders raced over to cut it off, but the best the right fielder could do was knock the ball down.

It was the center fielder backing up who finally fielded the ball and threw in to third. Jean, on her way around second, pulled up and slid safely back into second.

By this time the Dolphin bench was empty as every

player on the team rushed up to the foul line to watch and cheer. With the lead-off batter doubling, how could they fail to win this one?

But when Steve Deforrest struck out on a slow curve and Paul Swenson was only able to manage a feeble tap back to the mound, all of a sudden it did not seem so inevitable that the Dolphins were going to get Jean in from second base.

As Mike approached the plate, a rising tide of comments was sent his way from the Yankee stands, turning on the taunt that he couldn't even hit as well as his sister. But the riding only caused him to recall how well Jean had withstood the riding she had taken all during this game. He resolved grimly that he too would not let it bother him, certainly not the way it had the first time he had batted.

Shutting out the comments from the stands and the sly remarks of the catcher, he looked the first pitch over carefully and decided against swinging. It was just outside for a ball.

"That's the old eye!" called Paul DiAngelo from the bench. "Wait for the one you want!"

And that was precisely what Mike intended. The Yankee pitcher unwound and fired the ball plate-

119

ward. The ball appeared to be inside, but Mike tensed himself just in case the ball curved over the plate. And then he saw it begin to drift out over the plate. *Good!* He brought his bat around as quickly as he could, catching the ball out in front of him and snapping his wrists the moment he connected. The shock of the impact was a solid one, and Mike knew he had hit the ball well as he continued his follow-through and then started to dig for first.

Glancing up, he saw the ball dropping beyond the infielders and saw the outfielders racing over to cut the ball off. *A clean hit! And with two outs, Jean should have been running on the pitch!* As he crossed first, he looked back and saw that Jean had fallen rounding third.

The throw from center was already on its way, but Jean picked herself up and raced down the line for home. The throw bounced on the wrong side of the mound and then hopped over the mound and headed right for the Yankee catcher crouching in front of the plate. The moment the ball entered the catcher's glove, it seemed, Jean's sliding body crumpled into the catcher.

The catcher went over backward, and the ball went flying over his shoulder toward the backstop.

"Safe!" cried the umpire as he thrust both his palms out and down.

But Mike's jubilation and that of the team was shortlived as Jean continued to lie on the ground after the catcher for the Yankees picked himself up. Slowly, she raised herself to a sitting position and reached down to feel her left ankle.

There was a sudden hush in the ball park. For the first time that night, the stands behind the Yankee bench did not have a ready remark.

And how could they, Mike thought bitterly, after a slide like that? How could they still think that Jean should stick to softball or skipping rope?

He joined the group of Dolphin players running to Jean's side.

10

BY THE TIME they got Jean home, her left ankle had swollen considerably. But she could move all her toes and stand on the foot, somewhat gingerly. She hobbled about the house, grimacing with occasional pain whenever she allowed herself to come down too carelessly on the foot.

Propped up finally on the living room sofa with an unobstructed view of the television set, she grinned wryly and said, "There goes the end of a major league career."

Mr. Tobin laughed at his daughter. "You'll survive," he said. "It's a sprain, a mean one, but I used to get those all the time when I was a kid. Your mother's gone to get some ice. That should bring the swelling down. You'll be all right."

The phone rang.

"I'll get it," Mike's father said.

"That was a great slide, Jean," Mike said.

"I should have scored standing up, for crying out loud. Tangle-foot, that's what I am, a tangle-foot. Anyway, Mike, it was your single that drove me in."

Jean's mother hustled in with an ice pack. "I called the doctor," she told Jean. "He said to use plenty of ice and to come in Monday to his office so he can examine your ankle, and he also said to keep off of it."

By the time the ice pack was successfully fastened to the side of Jean's ankle with an elastic bandage, Mr. Tobin returned to the living room. "That was Channel Eleven," he told them. "They want to bring their cameras over tomorrow for a quiet interview at the house here."

"I don't want to be interviewed," said Jean.

"Me, neither," said Mike.

"They promised they wouldn't pester you, Jean. You're news. And they just want to know how you are. I told them around one o'clock."

"Well, *I* won't be here," said Mike.

His father smiled at him. "Good idea. It's Jean they want to interview—Jean and her sprained ankle."

Jean shook her head. "All this fuss," she said.

123

"And all I wanted to do was play a little baseball, for crying out loud."

Her father grinned down at her. "Well, you did play quite a bit of baseball, but everyone else was doing the crying out loud."

"What did you think of those signs?" Jean asked her father.

The man shrugged. "It's a free country. Everyone's got a right to protest whatever they want."

"Yes," Jean said, sighing wearily and leaning back on a pillow. "I guess they have at that."

And that was the only comment Jean allowed herself concerning the actions of that Yankee rooting section either then or later in front of Channel Eleven's TV cameras. Not very much of the interview got on the news program the next evening, since Jean simply refused to comment on any question she felt was inappropriate. She just looked at the reporter without responding at all and waited for the next question.

The only statements the station got that they were able to use was that Jean liked to play baseball very much and that she hoped her efforts helped the team to a winning season.

By Tuesday she was attending school on crutches, but by Wednesday she had discarded the crutches and was making it to school without them. But she limped painfully, and she made no effort at all to show up for the next two practice sessions and for the two games that were played that week.

Billy Cashman played third in Jean's absence, and the team lost both games by lopsided scores. Billy did his best to take Jean's place at third, and his arm was more than adequate for the long throw across the diamond. But he had difficulty holding onto the ball long enough to be able to make the throw.

All of a sudden, it seemed, the team realized as one man just what kind of a job Jean had been doing at the hot corner.

Two weeks after Jean's slide into home, the Dolphins were playing the Cubs, a team that had just overtaken them and was now in second place behind the Yankees. They had managed to push across four runs in the first inning, only to fall behind in the third when the Cubs scored six times after two costly errors —one by Billy Cashman at third and another by

125

Mike in right field, when Mike let what should have been a single get through his legs.

The error allowed three runs to score and came with two outs immediately after Billy Cashman had booted an easy roller and then thrown wildly to first.

Al Dekin finally caught a pop fly to end the scoring. As Mike trotted in, Paul DiAngelo fell in beside him and tried to cheer him up.

"Don't let that one get to you, Mike. You've been doing fine in right."

"I should have put one knee down. I was thinking about it, but I wanted to make a flashy pickup."

Paul smiled. "I know the feeling. I should get down on one knee more often myself."

"You don't have to worry, Paul."

"It can happen to any of us—if we're not careful, Mike."

As they reached the bench, Coach Franklin called Mike over to him. Mike tossed his glove toward the bench and headed for the coach. He had a hunch he knew what was coming.

"Mike, I'm taking you out," the coach said.

Mike felt a tightening in his stomach. He had guessed right. He nodded and turned back to the bench.

"Wait a minute, Mike."

Mike looked back at the coach.

126

"It's not because of that error, Mike," the coach said. "That was just a mechanical mistake. In the future just keep one knee down, and you'll be all right. I just want to try Lee Wagner at third. That means putting Billy Cashman back in right. And Skip hasn't played in two games, so I'm putting him in left in place of Lee Wagner. Nothing personal, okay?"

"Sure, Coach," Mike replied, feeling somewhat better and grateful to the coach for his consideration in attempting to reassure him. Still, that error of his *had* been damaging and could easily cost them this game.

If so, it would be the third loss in their last four starts.

Lee Wagner started off the top of the fourth with a sharp single, and everyone started talking about a rally. But Steve Deforrest sent a high hopper back to the pitcher who threw to second for the force on Lee. Bob Corbett then flied deep to the center fielder.

Two outs.

But then Paul Swenson and Billy Cashman walked to load the bases, and it looked as if a rally really was in progress as Skip Weismann dug himself in at the plate.

Skip watched the first pitch go by for a called strike.

"That's all right," called Paul DiAngelo. "Look them over. Wait for your pitch."

The next pitch to Skip was well outside, and Skip swung so hard he almost fell down. The bench fell silent. With two strikes and two outs, the runners would be going full out the moment that Skip swung.

Mike leaned forward anxiously on the bench. The Cub pitcher unwound and sent the ball plateward. It was a high pitch, and Mike wanted Skip to lay off it. But the fellow swung at it desperately and missed completely to end the threat.

In their half of the fourth, the Cubs went out in order with two fly balls to center and an easy roller to Al Dekin at second.

It was Al who led off the top of the fifth. He singled. Paul DiAngelo singled also. Pete Ceballo watched a slow curve miss the plate, then stepped into a fast ball and rammed it on a line into right center. The throw went in to the plate in an effort to stop Paul DiAngelo from scoring. But it was too late, and Pete ended up on second with a double.

A tie ball game!

Then Lee Wagner flied out, and Steve Deforrest struck out. Bob Corbett slashed a line drive right back to the Cub pitcher, who flung his glove up in self defense and made the third out.

The roof fell in during the bottom of the fifth as Lee Wagner came in too slowly for a grounder down the third base line and then hurried his throw to Steve at first. The throw was in the dirt, and Steve let it get by him.

The runner pulled up on second, and the next batter singled him home. Paul Swenson was a little upset by this and walked the next batter. With two men on he pitched very carefully to the next Cub batter and ran the count to three and two.

Then the batter lofted a high fly to left field. Mike watched it, expecting to see Skip Wiesmann drifting back to get under it. However, to his total astonishment, Skip was just standing in left field watching the ball.

Get back! Get back! he thought urgently, jumping to his feet.

Too late it occurred to Skip that the ball was going to fall behind him. He started to backpedal, his glove over his head. But the ball dropped well beyond him, and by the time Paul DiAngelo threw the ball in, two more runs had scored to make it nine to six in the Cubs' favor.

And that was the final score.

It was a dispirited bunch of ballplayers that were grouped about the bench after the game. There hadn't been many spectators, and it had not taken very long for the field to look empty. Empty and forlorn. And that, Mike realized, was precisely how each Dolphin player felt.

"Okay, fellows," said Coach Franklin, "cheer up. Remember, you can't win them all. Practice Monday at six. I'll expect to see you all there."

As the players began to move away, the coach spoke directly to Mike. "How's Jean, Mike?"

"I'm not sure," Mike replied honestly.

The players halted and turned to regard him and the coach. It seemed they too were interested in Jean's condition.

"What do you mean, Mike?" the coach asked. "Is Jean's ankle still bothering her or not?"

"I'm just not sure," Mike repeated.

Paul DiAngelo took a step toward Mike. "You mean Jean's foot may be all right, but she's not letting on?"

Reluctantly, Mike nodded. Yes, this was what he

meant, all right. Of late he had caught glimpses of Jean that revealed an almost complete lack of discomfort as she moved about the kitchen or across the room to adjust the television. More than once in the past week as she walked past his room while he was working at his desk, she had not seemed to favor her left foot at all.

Mr. Franklin was surprised. "Doesn't she want to play for the Dolphins?"

"I don't know," replied Mike.

"All that aggravation," remarked Paul DiAngelo. "I don't blame her."

"Is that it, Mike?" persisted Mr. Franklin. "Too much of a hassle?"

"I haven't spoken to her about it," Mike admitted. "I figure she'll tell me when she feels like it." He shifted uncomfortably under Mr. Franklin's questioning gaze. He hoped he had not been showing disloyalty by speaking like this.

"I see . . . well then I guess that goes for the rest of us as well. We'll just have to wait until Jean feels ready to confide in us. And of course, Mike, her ankle could still be sensitive, even though it may not appear so."

Mike nodded. That was why he had not told anyone else before this of his suspicions.

"If Jean decides not to play," spoke up Skip Weismann, "then we won't have to worry about our Little League charter, will we?"

Everyone turned to look at Skip, but it was Steve Deforrest who spoke up, "That's right. And we won't have to worry about winning so many games either."

The team broke up then, and as Mike started for home through the gathering darkness, he wondered if perhaps it wouldn't be a good idea to bring up the subject with Jean after all. As tonight's error revealed, he probably was not yet ready to play the outfield regularly for the Dolphins—despite Coach Franklin's kind words.

But there was no doubt at all about Jean—Little League charter or not, she belonged on third base!

11

THE NEXT AFTERNOON, a Sunday, Mike knocked on Jean's door.

"Come in," she called.

Mike pushed open the door and walked inside. He was wearing his baseball cap, his bat was resting on his shoulder, and a glove was dangling from the bat by its strap.

"Hi," he said. "How about some baseball?"

Jean was lying face down on her bed, reading a magazine. Her thick auburn curls hid completely the back of her dress to the waist. She had not changed from the dress she had worn to church, and she still had on her white shoes.

Jean rolled over onto her side and closed the magazine, keeping one finger in it to mark her place.

133

"Can't," she said. "Might reinjure my ankle. It still hurts some. But you go ahead, Mike. Should be someone at the ball park by this time. Steve, or Paul."

"Well then, how about a game of catch in the backyard?"

"No. You go ahead, Mike. I want to read this story in the magazine."

"You can read that any time. It's real nice out. Just right for a game of catch."

She looked out the window. It was as wide open as she could get it, and the long sheer curtains were billowing out from the gentle breeze, while the sounds of the summer afternoon came clearly though the open window. Pleasantly blended together were the constant murmur of cars passing in the streets below, a lawnmower cutting grass nearby, the chattering of birds in the tree just outside her window—and in the distance the clear shouts of children at play. Jean looked back at Mike.

"Just a game of catch?"

"A quiet game of catch in the back yard."

"Okay. Get out of here and let me change. I'll be right down."

Mike watched as Jean picked her way carefully down the back porch steps a moment later. He was not so sure all of a sudden that Jean's ankle was really okay.

"Now take it easy, Mike," Jean cautioned him as she walked past him over to a spot in front of the fence. "Don't make me go lunging all over the place for your pegs."

Mike nodded. "Okay," he said.

But that—after a deceptively quiet beginning—was precisely what Mike had in mind.

Their first throws were lazy and soft. Jean loosened up slowly, but soon began returning the ball to Mike with most of her old authority and with no sign that there was anything at all the matter with her left ankle. As a result Mike regained his earlier certainty that Jean was hiding the true condition of her ankle from him.

He burned one back at her without warning. Jean caught the ball in surprise. "Hey," she said, "watch that."

"Aw, come on. We're both playing like a couple of old ladies. Let's loosen up some."

"Well, I'm not an old lady," Jean retorted, and fired the ball back at Mike with such force that he winced as he caught it.

"That's more like it," grinned Mike, as he threw back at her, hard.

She caught the ball easily, smiling. "Is that the best

135

you can do?" she asked. Then she threw a scorcher at Mike.

He knocked the ball down, then picked it up quickly and said, "Bet you can't get this one."

He deliberately threw wild and to Jean's left. Without thinking—and without hesitation—she leaped for the ball, pushing off her left foot. Even as her glove brushed the ball, she cried out in sudden pain.

Forgetting the ball entirely, she collapsed upon the grass, her face twisted in an effort to keep herself from crying out a second time. She sat up quickly, reached back to her left ankle, and began massaging it, as if she were trying to push the pain back into the foot.

Jean looked up at Mike and tried a smile. "I knew I should have stayed in my room."

Mike felt terrible. He looked at her weakly, wondering how many different ways he should punish himself for what he had just done. "I'm sorry, Jean," he managed.

"Just a wild throw, Mike. I shouldn't have gone after it."

"It's all my fault. I thought your foot was better. I was testing you."

She looked at him for a long moment, still massaging her ankle. The color had returned to her face, and it was obvious that the pain in her ankle had already begun to subside. "Well that's fine. So now you know I really do still have a sprained ankle."

"But you've been walking without a limp."

"So I don't go around like I was crippled for life. I have to keep it tightly bandaged, and it is still sensitive."

"Would you like to take a baseball bat and beat me over the head with it?"

She got up slowly and grinned wickedly at him. "Don't you worry," she said. "I'll think of something. But first I'll let you sweat, wondering what it is I'm going to do to you."

As he started to move forward to help her, she waved him away, walked over gingerly, and picked up her glove. "Now let's finish this game of catch. But this time I mean it. No wild pegs. Okay?"

It was a chastened Mike who agreed to that condition and resumed the game of catch well into the afternoon until they were both called in for supper.

Supper was over, and Mike was up in his room puzzling over a model airplane he had finally decided to put together when the doorbell rang. He heard his mother pass down the hall under his room and answer the door. There was a soft mutter of voices, and

137

then his mother called up the stairs for Jean. Mike went back to his model.

About five minutes later he heard Jean's rapid knock on his door. He put down the plastic fuselage and called, "Come in."

Jean entered, carrying a roll of paper in her hand. "That was Steve Deforrest," she told him.

"What did he want?"

"He had something to give me."

Mike frowned.

"You mean you didn't know about it either?"

"Know about what?"

"This petition."

He looked again at the paper in her hand. "I didn't know anything about it, Jean. Honest."

She smiled. "It's really quite eloquent. Here's what it says: 'Dear Jean, we need you at third base. At least come down and watch us until your ankle gets better.' "

"Who signed it?"

"It looks like the whole team—and Mr. Franklin, too."

"I know why they did it, Jean."

"What do you mean?"

"Like me, they thought you'd had it with playing baseball. All that fuss and everything."

"So I was using my ankle as an excuse."

Mike nodded.

"Now I suppose that should make me really angry, Mike. But it doesn't. Because, you know? It *had* occurred to me, at that. But not for long, I promise. And this . . ." She held up the petition. "settles it. When's your next game?"

"Wednesday. Against the Yankees."

"The Yankees?"

Mike grinned. "That's right."

"I'll be there." She turned to leave his room; but as she reached the doorway, she paused and looked back at him. "Know what Paul DiAngelo wrote next to his signature?"

Mike shook his head.

"That he was a nut for voting the way he had."

She closed the door behind her.

There was just a normal crowd of spectators behind the Yankee bench as Mike approached the bench and dropped his glove upon it. And no big signs.

As Steve Deforrest approached, Mike said to him, "Looks like this game will be a lot quieter than the last one."

"Have you heard the news?"

"What news?"

"We're not getting an official Little League charter."

"Because Jean's on our roster?"

Steve shook his head. "We sent in our application too late for this season. That's what Mr. Franklin said. He said all the other coaches were afraid of something like this because they had to wait so long to get some of the team's organized."

"So all that fuss about Jean . . ."

"Yeah," Steve agreed. "Isn't that something?"

"Let's warm up."

To Mike's surprise, Jean arrived in her uniform just before the start of the game. He saw Coach Franklin welcome her and then walked over himself.

"Are you going to play?"

"That's up to Coach Franklin. Mom took me to the doctor's this afternoon, and he taped my ankle up real tight and said I could play if I was careful."

"Well, maybe you better not then. Remember what happened when I threw that ball wide to you."

"It feels a lot better, Mike."

Mike shrugged. "You sure kept that trip to the doctor's a secret."

140

"Well, a girl can't be always telling her brother everything all the time."

"Yeah. I suppose that's right."

To Mike's surprise, he heard Coach Franklin read his name off as a starter. Right field. When he heard Billy Cashman's position, he understood. Billy was to play third. Coach Franklin was not going to chance Jean's ankle at the hot corner for this game. Mike was relieved.

The Yankees were the home team for this game and, batting first, scored two quick runs on a single, a walk, and a double down the left field line. But Paul Swenson hung in and got the side out with no more damage.

The Dolphins didn't get those runs back until the second when Paul DiAngelo led off with a single and was doubled home by Pete Ceballos. When Lee Wagner struck out for the first out and Steve Deforrest sent a lazy fly to center for the second, Mike figured the rally was about played out. Then Bob Corbett clocked a fast ball for his first home run of the season. A moment later Paul Swenson got into the act himself with a single.

But Billy Cashman ended the rally with a line drive, that went straight back to the Yankee pitcher.

But three big runs had scored, and Mike took the field a moment later feeling quite good about it.

Swenson kept the ball low on the first Yankee batter, forcing him to ground to third. Billy came up with the ball cleanly and fired across the diamond. The throw was fast enough, but low. Steve stretched and dug the ball out of the dirt for the first out. Mike punched his glove. That had been a close one. Billy was really having trouble with that throw.

The second batter singled over short. Swenson walked the next batter and then grooved one to the Yankee power hitter, who strode smoothly into the pitch and lofted one to deep center.

Mike raced over to back Paul up as the center fielder fled deep for the ball. For a moment it looked to Mike as if Paul were going to make a sensational catch, but the ball fell just beyond the center fielder's outstretched glove. So close to the trees were they that the ball struck one on the first bounce. Paul missed the ball as it rebounded crazily past him, but Mike pounced on the ball, whirled, and fired home.

The batter was trying to go all the way, and Mike's throw was right on the money. It bounced once, then hopped into Bob Corbett's waiting glove. Bob put the tag on the sliding runner, and it was two outs. ·

A moment later Swenson struck out the fifth batter, and Mike trotted in, aware that once again they were behind the Yankees.

Mike was the lead-off batter in the top of the third. As he selected his bat, Coach Franklin stepped to his side. "Very nice peg to the plate, Mike. Keep up the good work and wait for a good pitch now. See if we can start something here."

As Mike dug himself in at the plate, he went over in his mind what the coach had told him. *Wait for a good pitch.* Yes, that was his trouble, all right. He was too anxious at the plate. He just couldn't seem to get himself to hold back, even though whenever he did manage to do so, he usually did get some kind of a hit.

The first pitch to him looked good, but he refused to swing at it. At the last moment the ball swung outside. The umpire called it a ball, and Mike bent down to get some dirt to rub on the bat's handle. The next pitch to him was a slow one and a little high. He was tempted, but the ball was out of the strike zone, so again he held back.

"Ball two!" the umpire called.

Mike moistened his lips. The pitcher was behind him now and would have to come in with something good. He dug his rear foot in and ignored the taunts

143

from the Yankeep bench that said he was just looking for a walk, that he didn't dare swing.

The Yankee pitcher went into his full windup and came around with his fastest pitch. Mike wanted to hit it, but the ball was a little too much inside. He pulled back reluctantly, and the ball zipped into the catcher's mitt well inside.

"Ball three!" the umpire called.

"That's the way to look them over, Mike!" shouted Paul DiAngelo.

Mike knew that he should take the next pitch. A walk was as good as a hit, especially to a lead-off batter. But he wanted to hit the ball. He knew he could hit this guy. But he remembered the coach's words to him and told himself to let the next one go by.

The Yankee pitcher again went into his full windup and threw what looked like a nice fat pitch right over the plate. But Mike had already made his decision. At the last possible moment the ball curved out and away, missing the plate entirely.

"Take your base!" the umpire said.

As Mike tossed his bat toward the bench, the players were already on their feet, clapping their hands and proclaiming a rally in progress.

But Al Dekin struck out on a wide curve. As Mike watched Al swing, he realized suddenly how wise

Coach Franklin's advice to him had been. He would have looked just as bad as Al if he had not made himself wait this pitcher out.

Paul DiAngelo was the next batter. He looked over two close pitches, then selected one that was shoulder high and over the plate and blasted it into center field. Mike was off and running as soon as Paul connected and pulled up on third as the throw came home.

Men on second and third, one out.

Pete Ceballo stepped into the batter's box and let two strikes get past him before he unloaded. The ball was hit high, but not too deeply into left field.

"Tag up!" said Bob Corbett, who was coaching at third. "Score after the catch!"

Mike hustled back to third and with one foot resting on the sack waited for the left fielder to make the catch. The fellow judged the ball perfectly, camped under it, reached up, and pulled the ball in.

"Go!" shouted Bob.

As Mike raced down the line he saw the Yankee catcher bracing himself for the throw. Mike dug harder. He saw the catcher's eyes following the ball's path and then saw him reach out for the ball. Mike launched his slide, feet first. He felt the ground slam up into his back and saw the catcher—the ball now in his glove—start to turn toward him.

That was when Mike hit him. The fellow went

145

reeling back, the ball shooting out of his glove. A second later, he felt the rubber plate sliding under his back.

"Safe!" cried the umpire.

A moment later Lee Wagner lined out to the second baseman, but Mike's run had tied it all up again.

It was still a tie ball game in the top of the sixth when Lee Wagner led off with a single to right field and Steve Deforrest walked to put two men on with no one out.

"Here's where we salt it away!" said Coach Franklin as he stalked in front of the bench. "Let's keep it going now!"

But Bob Corbett was obviously too intent on collecting another home run. He got under a fat pitch and lofted it high but not far into center field. The center fielder gathered it in for the first out.

"Okay, that's only one away! Keep it going!" the coach cried.

Paul Swenson took a called strike, then went for two bad pitches for the second out.

The coach swung around as Paul headed unhappily back to the bench. His eye caught Jean.

"Jean," he said, "get a bat! You're hitting for Billy Cashman."

146

For a moment Mike thought Jean was going to argue. But she said nothing and left the bench quickly and selected a bat as the coach went over to the plate umpire.

"How's your ankle, Jean?" Mike called.

She glanced at him as she straightened, a war club in her hand. "I wouldn't be here if I didn't think I could play," she said.

There was no trace of a limp as Jean moved around behind the catcher and stepped into the batter's box. The Yankee infielders made a lot of noise when they saw who it was, but Mike had the feeling that their hearts weren't really in it. Jean had beaten them once before.

Jean swung on the first pitch and looked really bad. That was when Mike realized for the first time how long it had been since Jean had worked out with the team or held a bat in anger.

Jean took the next pitch. It was over for a strike. She stepped out of the batter's box to rub some dirt on the palms of her hands. She took quite a razzing while she did this, but paid it no heed. Stepping back into the batter's box, she took one practice swing, then held herself ready.

The Yankee pitcher came out of his windup and fired the ball toward the plate. From where Mike was

147

standing, it looked like a strike all the way. But Jean did not offer at it.

"Ball!" called the umpire.

So that made it one and two.

"That's the eye!" Paul DiAngelo called. "That's the way to look them over!"

The next pitch was low, and the one after that was inside. Three and two, two outs and two men on. The runners would be off on the next pitch. Jean stepped out of the batter's box, looked out over the stands in back of their bench for a moment, then stepped back in.

Mike moved away from the bench, too tense to do much but watch. He didn't trust himself to shout anything. The Yankee pitcher came out of a full windup and sent his fastest pitch at the plate. It was right down the alley, and Jean swung, catching the ball solidly, slashing it over the second baseman's head into right field. It was well hit and kept skidding to the right away from the right fielder as the fellow chased it down the line.

Lee Wagner and Steve Deforrest had been off and running from the moment the ball left the Yankee pitcher's hand. Both scored standing up as Jean raced to second base with a pinch hit double.

And now it was Mike's turn to bat.

He picked out a fast ball and lined it into center field, where the center fielder moved in a few steps and caught it for the third out.

As he headed back to the bench, he expected to see Coach Franklin beckon to him. Jean would play third now, so that meant Billy Cashman would be put back in right field. Coach Franklin caught the uncertainty in Mike's eyes and shook his head at him.

"I figure you should stay in, Mike," the coach told him as Mike headed past him for his glove. "You've earned the right to finish this game, I figure."

As Mike took his position in right field, he tried to understand why—at this particular moment—the coach had come to that decision. And as he considered the question, he came to the conclusion that it was not so much that throw home in the third as much as it was the fact that he had waited out the Yankee pitcher that same inning for a walk, enabling him to score on Pete's fly ball to left later. He had shown the coach he could take instructions, that he could curb his urge to hit every pitch that came his way. This wasn't sandlot ball. This was Little League.

Paul Swenson struck out the first Yankee batter in the bottom of the sixth. Mike and Paul both shouted their approval from the outfield. With the score now six to four in their favor, they felt pretty confident that they were back on the winning track—again at the expense of the league-leading Yankees.

But the next Yankee batter poked one through the box for a single, and the batter after that sliced a clean single down the left field line. Swenson lost the next batter after running the count to three and two, and with this walk loaded up the bases.

All of a sudden, victory didn't seem so assured. Coach Franklin journeyed out to the mound to have a talk with his pitcher. After a few words the coach patted Swenson on the back and returned to the bench.

Mike leaned forward and waited for Swenson's pitch. It came hard and fast, and that was how the batter swung, sending a long, long one into deep right field. Mike was off at the crack of the bat, his eye on the ball as he galloped back. At first he didn't think he had much of a chance, but as he stretched his legs he found the ball slowing and growing steadily larger and knew he was in line to catch it. Turning about suddenly, he swept in under the ball and caught it in full stride.

Paul DiAngelo was racing over from center. "Third base!" he cried. "Third base! The runner left too soon!"

Without breaking stride, Mike threw the ball with all the power of his young right arm. The ball stayed low, skipped once on the infield dirt, then disappeared into Jean's glove. His sister was astride third base, and the instant she caught the ball, she stamped her foot on the bag. The runner, desperately trying to make it back to third, pulled up.

The game was over.

"Hey, wait up!" Mike called.

Jean stopped and turned around. "Are you sure you really want to be seen walking down the street with your own sister all the time?" She was smiling when she said this, and Mike realized that she still understood how it was with him.

"I don't mind anymore, because now we're both famous. That's some double-play combination we make—right field to third base. Paul DiAngelo said we must have practiced that play for weeks. I told him we had."

She smiled, and the two of them started to walk together down the street toward home. Mike didn't

151

want to get soupy about it, but he hoped Jean realized how pleased he was to have a friend so close to home again—especially one who could play baseball as well as he could, even if she was his sister.